Playing Cupid

STEPHANIE

Stephanie is determined to have a great Valentine's Day. So what if her date for the school dance cancelled on her? Instead, she's helping Michelle by throwing a cool Valentine's party for her fourth-grade class.

But somehow, everything goes horribly wrong with Michelle's party! The face-painter, the magician, and guy that Stephanie hired to dress up as Cupid all cancel on her! Now Stephanie has to find a way to fix everything—before Valentine's Day is a total disaster for everyone!

MICHELLE

Michelle thinks Stephanie is the coolest big sister. Especially after she volunteers to put together the most awesome Valentine's Day party of all time for Michelle's class!

Michelle wants to do something nice for Stephanie in return. And what better present could she get her sister than a perfect date for the John Muir Middle School Valentine's dance? So what if Michelle doesn't know much about dating and boys? She knows she can find the date of Stephanie's dreams by Valentine's Day—no sweat.

FULL HOUSE™: SISTERS books

Two on the Town
One Boss Too Many
And the Winner Is . . .
How to Hide a Horse
Problems in Paradise
Will You Be My Valentine?
Baby-sitters, Incorporated
  (Coming in March 2000)

Available from MINSTREL Books

FULL HOUSE™
Sisters

Will You Be My Valentine?

DIANA G. BURKE

A Parachute Press Book

Published by POCKET BOOKS
New York   London   Toronto   Sydney   Singapore

This book is a work of fiction. Names, characters, places and incidents are products of the author's imagination or are used fictitiously. Any resemblance to actual events or locales or persons living or dead is entirely coincidental.

A MINSTREL PAPERBACK *Original*

A Minstrel Book published by
POCKET BOOKS, a division of Simon & Schuster Inc.
1230 Avenue of the Americas, New York, NY 10020

A PARACHUTE PRESS BOOK

Copyright © and ™ 2000 by Warner Bros.

FULL HOUSE, characters, names and all related indicia are trademarks of Warner Bros. © 2000.

ISBN: 0-671-04086-3

First Minstrel Books printing February 2000

10 9 8 7 6 5 4 3 2 1

A MINSTREL BOOK and colophon are registered trademarks of Simon & Schuster Inc.

Printed in the U.S.A.

Will You Be My Valentine?

MICHELLE

Chapter 1

All right! I love Valentine's Day!"

Michelle grinned. Her teacher, Mrs. Yoshida, had just announced that their class Valentine's Day party would be held right after school in one week, next Friday.

Mrs. Yoshida smiled. "That's wonderful, Michelle, because it's your turn to have a parent host the party."

"It is?" Michelle blinked.

"Oh, *great*," Rachel Tilly muttered. She sat at the desk beside Michelle. Her expression was *always* sour and she was usually nasty to everyone. Michelle decided to ignore her.

1

"You can count on me, Mrs. Yoshida!" Michelle said. She hoped her dad would host the party, but if not, she was sure someone else in her big family would volunteer.

"Excellent, Michelle." Mrs. Yoshida held up a hand when the bell rang. Everyone was eager to leave for the weekend, but all the kids stayed seated. "Don't forget to bring your donations for the Valentine's Day party by Tuesday."

Michelle nodded. Everyone always contributed to pay for refreshments and supplies for class parties.

"Class dismissed," Mrs. Yoshida said.

Michelle jumped out of her seat and ran to her cubby to get her backpack. Cassie Wilkins and Mandy Metz, her two best friends, rushed over to her.

"Wow! This is so cool, Michelle!" Cassie cheered.

"Yeah!" Mandy chimed in. "I can't wait for your Valentine's Day party."

Michelle beamed as she slipped her arms into the straps on her backpack.

"Not that it's going to be much of a party," a voice said loudly from behind them.

Michelle turned and glared at Rachel. "What's that supposed to mean?" she asked.

"It means you don't have a mother to host your party," Rachel said. "So it's going to stink."

Michelle's heart lurched. Her mother had died a long time ago. Michelle was just a baby when it happened. It was so mean of Rachel to bring it up.

I'm not going to let her know how much that hurt! Michelle decided. *Even though it does.*

"No, I don't have a mother," Michelle said. "But I've got a father, an uncle, an aunt, and my dad's best friend. One of them will be glad to host the party."

When Michelle's mom died, her dad, Danny, asked his best friend, Joey Gladstone, and Uncle Jesse to move in with him. He needed help raising Michelle and her older sisters, D.J. and Stephanie. Since then, Uncle Jesse married Aunt Becky. Now the two of them had twin, four-year-old boys, Nicky and Alex.

"That's why I'm not expecting anything fabulous," Rachel sighed. "None of those people can do anything half as good as a mom

3

can. *Everyone* said my mom's Christmas party was the best ever!"

Michelle fumed. The Christmas party had been great. But that didn't mean her Valentine's Day party wouldn't be great, too!

"We'll be lucky to get grocery-store cookies and canned punch at Michelle's party," Rachel sneered.

Mandy's eyes flashed. "No way, Rachel. Michelle will have an awesome party, with all kinds of neat stuff."

"Yeah!" Cassie's blond ponytail bobbed as she nodded. "No matter which person Michelle gets to host it. Right, Michelle?"

"Absolutely!" Michelle crossed her arms and met Rachel's gaze.

"We'll see." Rachel flipped her long, dark hair over one shoulder and walked away.

"Don't worry, Michelle," Cassie said. "You'll show her."

Michelle frowned. *I had better show her!* she thought. *If the party is a flop, Rachel will tease me about it all the way through high school!*

The three friends walked toward the exit. After Cassie and Mandy said good-bye,

Michelle ran home. She was eager to ask her dad about hosting the party.

Danny and Aunt Becky co-hosted a morning TV show called *Wake Up, San Francisco.* Since Danny went to work earlier than most people, he got home earlier, too. Especially on Fridays. Michelle hoped she'd be able to talk to her father right away.

Michelle burst through her front door. "Hey!" Joey Gladstone almost dropped a stack of clean towels as Michelle flew in the door. She whizzed past him.

"What's the rush?" Joey asked.

"I have to talk to Dad about something really important." Michelle paused halfway up the stairs. "Is he home yet?"

"Not yet." Joey started up the stairs after her. "I'm here if you need me."

"Thanks. I'll let you know!" Michelle raced to the second floor and into the bedroom she shared with Stephanie. She tossed her backpack on her bed and changed into her old sneakers. Then she ran back downstairs to wait for her father.

The doorbell rang ten minutes later. Finally!

Michelle felt as if she had been waiting for *hours*! She threw open the door, expecting to see Danny with his arms full of groceries or stuff from work, but instead she found the paperboy.

"Oh. It's just you." Michelle's shoulders sagged.

"Yep. It's just me." The older boy smiled. "Collecting again."

"Oh, yeah. I'll go get—" Michelle's face lit up when she saw Danny coming up the front walk. "Dad! It's about time!"

"Hi, Michelle." Danny winked at Michelle, then turned to the paperboy. "Is it collection time again?" He hesitated. "I'm sorry. I don't remember your name."

"It's Kevin, Mr. Tanner. Kevin Logan."

"Kevin." Danny nodded and pulled his wallet out of his suit coat. "Three dollars and fifty cents, right?"

"Yes, sir. That's right." Kevin took off his baseball cap and smoothed back his brown hair.

Hurry up! Michelle thought. She tapped her foot.

"There you go." Danny handed Kevin a five-dollar bill. "Keep the change."

"Thanks, Mr. Tanner!" Kevin flipped his cap back on and pocketed the money. Then he jumped off the porch and picked up his bike. "Bye, Michelle!"

"What a nice kid." Danny waved as Kevin rode away.

"Dad!" Michelle tugged on Danny's coat sleeve. "I have to tell you about something. It's really serious!"

"Then I guess we'd better talk." Danny followed Michelle into the house, and glanced at his watch. "Uh-oh."

"Uh-oh?" Michelle tensed. "What uh-oh?"

"I'm sorry, Michelle," Danny said, "but I have to make an important phone call. I'll be just a few minutes. Promise."

"But—" Michelle threw up her hands as Danny hurried into the kitchen. She didn't want anything else to distract him after his phone call. She sat at the kitchen table so she could catch him as soon as he hung up.

"Hello, Ms. Stuart," Michelle heard her father say. "This is Danny Tanner from *Wake Up*,

San Francisco." Danny nodded. "Yes, uh-huh. So you talked to our producer?"

Michelle glanced at the kitchen clock. She had never realized how slowly the second hand moved.

"That's right. We're taping a remote Valentine's Day segment and your sidewalk café is the perfect location." Danny laughed. "That's great! I'll see you with my crew at three-thirty next Friday afternoon!"

Three-thirty next Friday! Michelle gasped. The class party was from three to four next Friday! Her dad couldn't be on location *and* at her school at the same time!

Danny hung up and walked over to Michelle. "Okay, honey. I'm all yours. Now, what's on your mind?"

"Uh—" Michelle stared at Danny. He would *have* to do the Valentine taping for his TV show no matter what, she knew. It was his job.

Michelle also knew her father would feel awful if he had to turn down hosting her class party. She didn't want him to feel bad, so maybe—maybe it wasn't worth telling him about the party at all. "Umm—nothing," she said.

"Nothing?" Danny frowned, puzzled. "It sure didn't seem like nothing a minute ago."

"No, I—I had this problem, but I just figured out how to solve it for myself!" Michelle covered. "Thanks, Dad!"

"Sure, Michelle. Anytime." Danny scratched his head. He looked totally confused.

Michelle bolted from the kitchen. She hadn't really lied. She had just figured out that she needed to ask someone else to host her class party.

Joey! Michelle climbed the stairs two at a time. *What about Joey?* she thought. He was a very funny comedian who could always make her laugh with his weird voices and jokes. He knew a lot of cool games, too. Maybe he'd even wear a clown costume! She could help him shop for the refreshments and party favors.

Joey had just finished putting the towels away and straightening the linen closet. Michelle paused to catch her breath.

"Hey, Michelle." Joey shut the closet door and gave her his full attention. "What's up?"

Michelle hesitated. After what had just happened with her father, she decided to take a different approach. *Just in case.* "Are you doing anything special next Friday afternoon?"

"As a matter of fact, I am," Joey said.

"You are?" Michelle struggled to hide her disappointment.

"Yep. Your uncle Jesse's band is playing at a big Valentine's Day dance downtown Friday night and I'm going to be the emcee." He paused. "Neat, huh?" he asked in his hip-dude voice.

Michelle nodded.

"But," Joey continued, "we have to get all our stuff set up by four o'clock Friday afternoon. So we don't disrupt the fancy dinner that takes place before the dance starts."

"So Uncle Jesse's busy, too?" Michelle asked.

"Yep." Joey frowned. "Why?"

"Oh, no reason." Michelle forced a smile.

"Come on, Michelle." Joey raised an eyebrow. "You must have a reason for asking."

"Well, yeah." Michelle told him about needing someone to host her class Valentine's

Day party. "Dad can't do it because he has a taping for *Wake Up, San Francisco.* And now you and Uncle Jesse have to set up the band equipment."

"Wow, Michelle, I'm really sorry." Joey sighed.

"That's okay," Michelle told him. It wasn't his fault he had other plans. "Besides, I bet Aunt Becky would love to do it!"

Joey sighed again. "I bet she would, too, except that Becky is in charge of the twins' pre-school Valentine's Day party next Friday afternoon."

"Is the twins' party from three to four?" Michelle hoped it was earlier. She crossed her fingers for luck, but it didn't do any good.

"I'm afraid so." Joey shrugged.

Now what? Michelle wondered. All the adults in the house were busy!

"D.J.!" Michelle grinned as her oldest sister came down the hall with her arms full of books. D.J. was nineteen and in college. That was practically grown-up. Grown-up enough to handle a fourth-grade party, anyway.

11

"Hi, Joey. Hi, Michelle." D.J. smiled as she walked past them.

Michelle followed her sister into her bedroom. "Can I talk to you a minute, D.J.?"

"Sure." D.J. dropped her books and shoulder bag on the desk, then sat down on her desk chair. She leaned forward attentively. "What's up?"

"I have a problem," Michelle began. She perched on the edge of the bed and quickly explained about the party. "Can you do it, D.J.? Can you organize the party? It's only for an hour after school, and I'll help with everything."

"Sure. It might be fun." D.J. checked her calendar. "As long as it's not next Friday. I've got an incredibly important zoology exam at three o'clock, and I can't miss it."

Michelle just stared. She couldn't believe it! Everyone had plans for next Friday afternoon that couldn't be changed. Even D.J.! There wasn't anyone left to ask.

What am I going to do? Michelle wondered.

STEPHANIE

Chapter 2

I'm so excited, I can't stand it!" Stephanie sat across from her best friends, Allie Taylor and Darcy Powell, in a booth at the local pizzeria. Everyone hung out there, and today the pizzeria was jammed. Everyone was talking about the middle school's Valentine's Day party at the roller rink.

"This party is going to be *so* excellent! I love the roller rink."

"Me too!" Allie's eyes shone. "This may be the best party we've ever gone to!"

Stephanie grinned over at Darcy. Hmmm. She didn't seem too enthusiastic. The three girls had been friends for a long time, and Darcy was never this quiet. "What's the matter, Darce? Aren't you happy? This skating party is going to be the biggest event of the year!"

"I know." Darcy sighed and propped up her chin in her hands. "It's just that you and Allie have *dates* for the skating party."

"Dates?" Judy Morton was walking by their booth. She stopped abruptly.

Stephanie looked up. Judy had moved to San Francisco from Los Angeles a couple of months ago. She was pretty with long, auburn hair, and she always dressed in the latest styles. Judy seemed friendly enough and had become instantly popular. Still, there was something about the girl that bothered Stephanie. She just couldn't figure out what.

"Who are your dates for the skating party?" Judy asked. Her blue eyes glittered with curiosity.

"I'm going with Chris Morgan," Allie said.

"Chris Morgan?" Judy shrugged. "Never heard of him. Guess he's not on the football team. My boyfriend, Jeff, is the quarterback."

"We know," Stephanie said, slightly annoyed. She wasn't sure, but it sounded like Judy thought only athletes were worth dating.

Judy smiled at Stephanie. "Who's *your* date?"

"Sean Mason," Stephanie said. "He asked me a couple of weeks ago. Right after the skating party was announced."

Judy frowned. "I don't think I know him, either. Does Sean play football?"

"No." Stephanie bristled. Judy had set her sights on Jeff Perdue, the team's star quarterback, shortly after she arrived at John Muir Middle School. They started hanging out together almost immediately. Everyone thought they were the perfect couple.

"Sean is a scientific genius," Stephanie said. "And he's the president of the chess club. He doesn't have time to play sports."

"He's gorgeous, too," Darcy added.

"Oh." Judy shrugged. She obviously wasn't impressed.

How rude! Stephanie thought.

"What about you, Darcy?" Judy asked.

"I don't have a date yet," Darcy said.

So that's what's bothering her! Stephanie glanced at her friend. Darcy shifted position under Judy's pointed gaze.

"Well, don't worry, Darcy," Judy said. "The Valentine's Day party isn't until next Friday. That's a whole week away. Maybe you'll get lucky by then."

Lucky? Stephanie frowned. She couldn't tell if Judy was trying to be encouraging or if she had just cleverly implied that Darcy didn't have much hope of getting a date.

"Oh, there's Jeff!" Judy waved as her tall, blond boyfriend came in the door. "Got to go."

Darcy shook her head as Judy rushed off. "Is it my imagination, or did Judy just insult me?"

"It's hard to tell," Stephanie said.

"Yeah, it sure is." Allie turned to Darcy. "I thought you wanted to go to the skating party with Rusty Anderson."

"I do, but he hasn't asked me," Darcy said.

"Then why don't you ask him?" Stephanie took a sip of her soda and glanced toward the door, looking for Sean. He had said he was going to stop by after he ran an errand for his mom. She didn't see him anywhere.

"Normally I would, but this is the *Valentine's* Day party. It wouldn't be the same if I did," Darcy explained.

Stephanie had to agree. She would have asked Sean, but she was thrilled when he asked her first.

"I'm positive that Rusty likes you, Darcy," Allie said. "But maybe he's afraid to ask you. Because he doesn't know if you'll say yes."

"Rusty is kind of shy, but I've got an idea." Stephanie grinned and leaned forward.

"What?" Darcy asked.

"You have to make it easy for him to ask you," Stephanie said. "Just get him into a conversation and casually mention the skating party. That will give him an opening."

"Right!" Darcy brushed a dark curl off her forehead. "And I'll drop a lot of hints so he knows I *really* want to go with him."

"That might work." Allie grinned.

"Great!" Stephanie sat back. Her friend's problem was taken care of. She looked at her watch. "Whoops! I can't believe we've been here over an hour! I've got to get home. I want to get my homework done tonight so I have the rest of the weekend totally free."

"I'd better get going, too." Allie slid out of the seat and picked up her books. "Are we still on for the mall tomorrow?"

"Absolutely," Stephanie said. "I want to get a new outfit to wear next Friday."

"Is two o'clock okay?" Allie stepped back so Darcy could get out of the booth. "My mom will drive."

"Works for me," Stephanie said. "What about you, Darcy?"

"Well, I guess it couldn't hurt to be prepared." Darcy slung her backpack over her shoulder. "I mean, if Rusty doesn't ask me to the skating party, I can always use a new outfit."

"He'll ask you, Darcy! Think positively." Allie led the way through the crowd toward the door.

"Why don't you just call Rusty tonight?" Stephanie suggested. "You could pretend it's about a homework assignment or something."

"I think I will," Darcy said.

As they drew closer to Judy and Jeff's table, Stephanie saw Judy glance toward them and whisper in Jeff's ear. She suddenly had the uneasy feeling that Judy was talking about her and her friends.

Am I just being paranoid? Stephanie wondered. It wasn't as if she and Darcy and Allie had any deep, dark secrets.

Then Stephanie saw Sean through the front window. So what if he wasn't a jock? she thought. He *was* extremely cute with dark brown hair and startling blue eyes. She couldn't help but feel a little smug when he walked into the pizzeria and headed straight for her. From the corner of her eye Stephanie could see that Judy was watching with intense interest.

"Hi, Sean!" Stephanie smiled. "I was just leaving, but—"

"Whew! Then I'm glad I caught you," Sean said. "I've got some bad news."

"I don't like the sound of that," Darcy muttered with a worried glance at Stephanie.

Neither do I! Stephanie braced herself. "What's wrong?"

19

"Are you sick or something, Sean?" Allie asked.

"No." Sean shook his head, then sighed again. "My mom just told me that we're going out of town next weekend. Right after school on Friday afternoon!"

"Next weekend?" Stephanie asked. She hoped she hadn't heard him right.

Sean nodded. "I won't be able to go to the Valentine's Day party at the roller rink." He paused and lowered his gaze. "I'm really sorry."

Stephanie stood there, silent. She felt completely stunned. A long, awkward moment passed before she collected herself. It wasn't like Sean was breaking their date because he wanted to, she told herself. He seemed as upset as she felt.

"That's okay, Sean. I totally understand." Stephanie managed a weak smile, but inside she was panicking.

Where am I going to ever find another Valentine's Day date?

MICHELLE

Chapter
3

Michelle stared at the TV in the living room. She wasn't really watching the rerun of the old sitcom. In fact, she didn't even have the sound turned up. All she could think about was her class's Valentine's Day party—and the fact that *nobody* in her family could host it!

There's only one thing to do, Michelle decided. Mrs. Yoshida would understand when she explained the problem. The teacher would just ask someone else to take her turn.

But Rachel won't understand. She'll jump on the chance to give me a hard time! Michelle thought.

She flopped over and rested her head on the arm of the sofa. She was so depressed, she didn't even look up when Stephanie came in and dropped her backpack on the coffee table.

"*Hello*, Michelle," Stephanie said after a few seconds of silence. "Am I invisible, or what?"

"Sorry, Stephanie." Michelle sat up and sighed. "Hi."

"Looks like you feel about the same way I do right now." Stephanie frowned and sat down. She dropped a copy of her school's newspaper on top of her backpack. "Did you flunk a math test or something?"

Michelle shook her head and stared at the TV remote in her hand. "Worse."

Stephanie sighed. "I know the feeling." Another moment passed before she asked, "What's your problem?"

"The problem is my class Valentine's Day party next Friday." Michelle waved the TV remote and spoke in a frantic rush. "It's my turn to have someone in my family host it. Only everybody in *this* family is busy next Friday! I'm sure my teacher would give it to someone else and let me take another holiday party, but—"

"But?" Stephanie prompted when Michelle paused to breathe.

"But Rachel Tilly would *never* let me forget it if I passed the party on to someone else!" Michelle fumed. "It's not my fault I don't have a mom to take care of these things."

Stephanie's eyes narrowed. "What do you mean? Did Rachel tease you about not having a mother?"

"She did today," Michelle said.

"Oh! That is so unfair!" Stephanie's expression darkened. "And mean!"

"Tell me about it," Michelle responded. She stared at her sister a moment.

Hey! Wait a minute! she thought. Stephanie was in grade school once. Maybe she could ask Stephanie for some advice about this whole Rachel thing.

"Steph," Michelle started. "What did you do about the no-mom problem when you were in fourth grade? Like when Dad and Uncle Jesse or Joey couldn't host a class party."

"I never had that particular problem. One of

23

them was always ready, willing, and able to do it." Stephanie glared straight ahead. Her expression was totally intense. "But the party's really not the problem, is it?"

Michelle recognized Stephanie's "fighting mad" look. Her cheeks were turning red, her mouth was pressed into a tight line, and her hands were clenched into tight fists. Michelle almost expected to see smoke coming out of her ears, too.

"*Rachel* is the problem," Stephanie said.

"Sort of." Michelle put the remote on the coffee table and scowled. "I'm not too thrilled about having to tell Mrs. Yoshida that nobody in my family can do the party, either."

"Well, don't worry, Michelle. You won't have to." Stephanie crossed her arms and smiled.

Uh-oh. Michelle knew *that* look, too. It was the look Stephanie got whenever she had one of her brilliant ideas. And Stephanie's brilliant ideas usually got her into *big* trouble.

"*I'll* do it!" Stephanie's grin widened.

"Do what?" Michelle asked.

Will You Be My Valentine?

"I'll host your class Valentine's Day party!" Stephanie exclaimed.

"You will?" Michelle hadn't thought of asking Stephanie, but now that her sister had volunteered, she thought it was a great idea.

Stephanie nodded. "And it will be fantastic." She locked eyes with Michelle. "We'll show Rachel Tilly that you don't need a mom to throw the best valentine party a fourth grade ever had."

"Wow, Stephanie! Thanks!" Michelle had no doubt that Stephanie would do a terrific job. The Tanner family reputation was at stake, and Stephanie had decided to defend it. As a rule, Stephanie had loads of enthusiasm. Best of all, at thirteen, Stephanie wasn't so much older than Michelle. She probably remembered better than any mom what fourth-graders liked to do for fun!

"I'm already getting some awesome ideas," Stephanie said. "How would you like it if Cupid himself made an appearance?"

"I would definitely like it." Michelle beamed.

"I hope there's a class collection to pay for

refreshments and stuff." Stephanie pulled a notebook and pencil out of her backpack.

"There is," Michelle assured her. "You can pick up the money after school on Tuesday."

Michelle hesitated, then added, "I would have asked you to host my party, Stephanie, but I thought you'd be busy next Friday for sure."

"Oh, well—" Stephanie shrugged, and her smile dimmed a little. "I *was* busy, but I'm not anymore. Except for your party, of course."

"You mean you had plans and now you don't?" Michelle asked.

"Yeah." Stephanie flipped to a blank page in the notebook and wrote something down.

"What happened?" Michelle asked. Now that her problem had been solved, she realized that Stephanie *had* looked kind of down when she first came in. Michelle had just been too worried about her own troubles to notice.

"Sean Mason was my date for the middle school Valentine's Day party at the roller rink next Friday," Stephanie explained. "He had to cancel. He just found out that his family is going out of town that day." Stephanie paused to take a deep breath, then smiled at Michelle. "Lucky for you, though! Otherwise I wouldn't be able to host *your* party."

Stephanie's happy face didn't fool Michelle. Her sister was really upset. Michelle frowned. It didn't seem right that she was going to get her class party because of Stephanie's bad luck.

"You could still go to the roller rink, Stephanie," Michelle said. "You don't have to have a date, do you?"

Stephanie sat back with an shocked expression. "Go to a *Valentine's* Day party alone? No way!" She leaned forward. "Besides, I really do want to help you out with your class party, Michelle. Honest."

"Okay." Michelle didn't argue, but she still felt bad for Stephanie. She picked up the remote and turned up the volume on the TV.

"What time is this party taking place, anyway?" Stephanie asked. "Do I need an excuse from Dad to get out of school?"

"No. It's after school, from three to four." Michelle cast a sidelong glance at Stephanie. "What time is the skating party?"

"It starts at four," Stephanie said.

Four! Inspiration struck Michelle like a bolt of lightning. She was bubbling over with excitement as she turned to Stephanie. "Hey! What if I found you a date? Then you could do both! My party *and* the skating party!"

"You? Find *me* a date?" Stephanie shook her head. "Oh, no. No. Just forget it, okay?"

"Why? You're helping me. Now I want to help you!" Michelle insisted. *Why does Stephanie have to be so stubborn sometimes?* she wondered.

"First of all, you don't have the slightest idea what kind of guy I'd *want* to date," Stephanie explained. "And second, even if you did have a clue, how could you possibly find him? I appreciate the thought, but you're way too young to be playing Cupid."

"No, I'm not. I—" Michelle started to protest. Then the headline on Stephanie's middle school newspaper caught her attention.

Find a Valentine
in Tuesday's Special Issue

"What's this?" Michelle picked up the paper and pointed to the headline.

Stephanie rolled her eyes. "The editor decided it would be cool to let kids place free personal ads for Valentine's Day."

"What's a personal ad?" Michelle thought she knew, but she wanted to be sure.

"Things like 'Short seventh-grade boy looking for short seventh-grade girl who likes fishing.'" Stephanie grinned, then went back to jotting down her party ideas.

"Why don't you put in an ad, Stephanie?" Michelle asked. "For someone to take you to the skating party? Then you won't have to miss all the fun."

Stephanie gasped. "No way!"

"Why not?" Michelle frowned. "Is it too late?"

"No, it's not too late," Stephanie told her. "But let's just say it's not my thing. I would never use a personal ad to get a date."

"Oh." Michelle stared at the phone number in the short article below the headline and memorized it. The deadline to place an ad was six o'clock that evening.

Stephanie picked up her notebook and backpack. "I'll be upstairs if you get any ideas. You know, like games and party favors. Anything you think the other kids would really like—just let me know and I'll get to work on it."

"Okay." Michelle just smiled. She had a great idea, but it didn't have anything to do with her class party.

"Can I have my newspaper back?" Stephanie held out her hand.

"Sure." Michelle gave Stephanie the paper.

As soon as Stephanie reached the top of the stairs, Michelle dashed for the kitchen phone and dialed. "Hello? Is this the right number to put a free Valentine ad in the special school paper?"

Michelle grinned. *Yes! I am totally going to find the perfect Valentine date for Stephanie!*

STEPHANIE

Chapter
4

Stephanie checked her reflection in the mirror and nodded with satisfaction. Her shining blond hair swung just right when she tossed her head, and her smoke-blue sweater complemented her tan jeans and brown shoes. *Casual and classy! Perfect!*

Stephanie finished with a touch of lip gloss. The mall would be swarming with kids hanging out on a Saturday afternoon. She wanted to look great just in case she ran into any cute boys who liked to roller-skate and weren't busy next Friday. *Which isn't likely—but it can't hurt to be prepared,* she thought.

"Darcy and Allie are here," Michelle called up the stairs.

Stephanie called back, "Tell them I'll be right down, okay?"

"Sure." Michelle ran upstairs and lounged against the bathroom door frame. "Where are you going?"

"The mall," Stephanie said. "I've got to find out how much Valentine favors and craft supplies for your party will cost."

"Cool!" Michelle grinned. "Can I go?"

"Not today, but I'll take you with me when I go to pick everything up next week, okay?" Stephanie expected Michelle to plead with her to change her mind. Instead, she just shrugged and smiled.

"Okay. You better hurry up, though." Michelle nodded toward the stairs. "Darcy and Allie look really excited about something."

They do? Stephanie grabbed her shoulder bag and raced down the stairs. She was dying of curiosity. Allie and Darcy rushed her out of the house. Something was definitely up.

"You'll *never* guess what happened!" Darcy

exclaimed as they headed down the front walk. Allie's mom was waiting in the car parked at the curb.

"What?" Stephanie asked. "Is it good or bad?"

"Both," Darcy reported. "I called Rusty about our history assignment like you suggested. And it worked! He asked me to go to the skating party with him!"

"Awesome!" Stephanie gave Darcy a thumbs-up.

"Yeah, but Rusty didn't ask in time to stop the nasty rumor that's going around," Allie said.

"*What* nasty rumor?" Puzzled, Stephanie shifted her gaze between the two girls.

Allie held her finger to her mouth when they neared the car. "We'll tell you when we get to the mall. It's too personal to talk about in front of my mom."

"Okay, so what's all this about a rumor?" Stephanie asked as Allie pushed through the door into the mall. She couldn't believe *anyone* could possibly have *anything* bad to say about

Darcy. Wondering about it had driven her crazy on the short ride to the mall.

Allie motioned Stephanie and Darcy to a bench under a leafy shade tree. "Want me to tell her, Darcy?"

"Yeah. Go ahead." Darcy seemed to deflate as she sank onto the wooden seat. "It's just so upsetting."

"What is?" Stephanie thought she would explode if somebody didn't tell her soon.

"I had three phone calls right after dinner last night," Allie said. "From Susie Michaels, Andrea Kraft, and Leslie Collins. I don't even know Leslie that well. But all of them wanted to know why Darcy couldn't get a date for the skating party. They made it sound like Darcy had some kind of infectious disease, or had done something terrible so no boy would ask her!"

"Whoa! How did they know Darcy didn't have a date in the first place?" Stephanie asked. She, Darcy, and Allie weren't close friends with any of those girls. Stephanie couldn't imagine why they would be interested in Darcy's social life.

"They all said Judy Morton made a point of telling them that Darcy couldn't get a date before they left the pizzeria yesterday," Allie reported. "And who knows how many other people she told!"

"That rat!" Stephanie wondered if that's what Judy had been whispering to Jeff, too.

"Why would she do that?" Darcy asked. She looked devastated.

"Just to be mean, I guess," Stephanie said. "But you'll have the last laugh."

"She will?" Allie blinked.

"Sure!" Stephanie raised an eyebrow. "Since Darcy's going to the Valentine's Day skating party with Rusty, she obviously *does* have a date. Everyone will think Judy was lying."

"Right!" Allie laughed. "Maybe *that* will teach her not to gossip about other people."

"Whew! Yeah. Everyone will see that the rumor isn't true!" Darcy placed her hand on her chest and sagged with relief.

Stephanie frowned. Judy had been watching and listening when Sean had broken *their* date! What on earth would Judy do with that information?

After she agreed to meet her friends in the same spot in an hour, Stephanie went to price party supplies while Darcy and Allie hunted for new outfits.

Stephanie already had a good idea of what she wanted for Michelle's party and where to look. When she left the craft and hobby store half an hour later, she was almost finished.

She had a list and prices for everything she needed to make great valentines. "Cupid" could hand them out. And she found paper cups with cartoon pictures and funny sayings at a party specialty store. Even the boys would like those. On Monday after school, she could go to the grocery store to price cupcakes, valentine candy, and something to drink.

"Which only leaves renting the Cupid costume. And talking Ronny Harkin into wearing it!" Pleased with her progress, Stephanie headed for the costume shop.

Stephanie had left a message on Ronny's answering machine that morning. She was hoping he'd call her back soon. He was the eighth-grade class clown, and she knew he was saving to buy a new mountain bike. She was sure he'd agree to play Cupid for ten dollars, especially since he wouldn't have to miss the skating party to do it.

Ronny wasn't the kind of guy who would be embarrassed to dress up like a fat baby with wings in a diaper. In fact, he'd probably love to do it. Still, she wouldn't relax until he agreed. *She* certainly didn't want to dress up in that silly costume!

"Anyone here?" Stephanie called out when she entered the costume shop.

"Coming!" An elderly man walked slowly out of a back storeroom and smiled. "I don't move as fast as I used to, but since this is the slow season, guess it doesn't matter much."

"I've got plenty of time." Stephanie quickly scanned the costumes displayed on the walls. The shop carried everything from realistic historical outfits to the most popular superheroes. But she didn't see anything that remotely resembled Cupid.

"What can I do for you?" The old man adjusted his glasses and leaned on the counter.

"I want to reserve a Cupid costume for next Friday," Stephanie said. "But I have to pick it up Wednesday or Thursday. Does that cost extra?"

"Nope. No extra charge. Cupid, you said?" The old man frowned and rubbed his chin. "What size?"

Stephanie blinked. She didn't know what size Ronny Harkin wore. "I'm not sure."

"They come in three adult sizes. Small, medium, and large," the old man said.

"Oh." Stephanie shrugged. Ronny was about her height but heavier. "What size would I wear if it fit loosely?"

"Medium should do it." The old man started back toward the storeroom. "Hope I have one. There isn't much demand for Cupid anymore."

While she waited for the clerk to find the costume, Stephanie wandered around the shop. A mannequin wearing an eighteenth-century dress in the window display caught her eye. She walked over to take a closer look at the elaborate white wig and gorgeous red gown.

Stephanie jumped when she heard a tap on the glass. She scowled when she saw

Judy Morton staring at her through the window.

Judy smiled and waved as the elderly man shuffled out of the storeroom again.

Stephanie wanted to tell Judy she was a total loser for gossiping about Darcy, but she didn't want to make a scene. She gave Judy a halfhearted wave and turned away as the old man stepped in front of the counter. The Cupid costume he held up stopped her cold.

"Found one!" The old man chuckled. "Easy to see why there's not much demand for Cupid, huh?"

I'll say! Stephanie stared. A padded diaper with a huge safety pin in front was fastened to an even more padded long-sleeved, flesh-toned leotard. There was also a long, leather case filled with arrows on a strap that was worn over the shoulder and across the chest. The arrow tips were shaped like hearts. Sheer white fabric stretched over wire, forming wings on the back. A small bow and a leafy head wreath with hearts on it completed the outfit.

"Let's see if this fits," the old man said.

"Fits?" Before Stephanie could back off, the old man held the costume up in front of her.

"Oh, my!" Stephanie heard someone say. She turned her head and saw Judy and Jeff walking into the shop. Judy covered her mouth to smother her giggles. "Oh, Stephanie. No wonder Sean dumped you!"

"Dumped me?" Stephanie's eyes flashed. "Sean *didn't* dump me, Judy!"

Judy didn't seem to hear. "I wouldn't want to go to the school skating party with someone dressed like Cupid, either! What a lame idea!"

"Come on, Judy." Jeff took Judy's arm and hauled her back out into the mall.

"No! Wait!" Stephanie waved her hands in a panic. "This is for my sister's—"

The door banged closed behind them.

"Class party." Stephanie's voice trailed off. "Not for me."

"Is there a problem?" the old man asked.

Problem? Problem? This is a catastrophe! Stephanie thought. Yesterday Judy couldn't wait to tell everyone that Darcy didn't have a date for the Valentine's Day party. *This* was a hundred times more embarrassing. Judy was probably heading for the nearest phone to call everyone she knew right now!

Stephanie put her head in her hands. *By Monday everyone at school will think Sean Mason dumped me because I'm going to the roller rink dressed as Cupid! The entire school is going to think I'm a complete nerd!*

Chapter
5

Michelle woke up Sunday morning wishing it was Monday. She was eager to see her ad in the valentine edition of Stephanie's school newspaper.

Stephanie would definitely bring a copy of the paper home. Danny loved to see the articles Stephanie wrote for it.

Michelle kept her ad a secret from everyone in the family, because Stephanie had told her to forget about finding a Valentine's Day date. If she found out Michelle was still trying, she might get mad all over again.

Michelle wandered down the stairs. She

42

smelled breakfast cooking in the kitchen, but her father was sitting on the front porch steps.

"Hi, Dad. What are you doing here?"

"Waiting for the newspaper." Danny smiled. "Aunt Becky's making breakfast this morning. Sausage and pancakes."

"Yeah." Michelle sniffed the air. "It smells great."

"There's Kevin now." Danny stood up and waved as Kevin stopped his bike at the end of the walk.

"Morning, Mr. Tanner!" Kevin pulled a paper out of his carrier bag, drew his arm back, and threw it.

Stephanie stuck her head out the front door. "Breakfast is ready!"

"Be right there!" Danny caught the paper and held it up. "Thanks, Kevin!"

Kevin smiled. "How are you doing, Michelle?"

"I'm okay." Michelle waved.

"Come on, you guys! Breakfast is getting cold." Stephanie ducked back inside. Kevin rode away.

Michelle followed Danny into the kitchen and sat down.

Ordinarily, nobody read the paper at the breakfast table, but Joey noticed that the *San Francisco Chronicle* had a special valentine personal section.

Just like Stephanie's school paper, Michelle thought. Except that all the responses in Stephanie's paper were sent by e-mail, not by letter.

"These are too funny." Joey laughed and set down his fork.

"What?" Uncle Jesse looked up from cutting Nicky's sausage into bite-size pieces.

"The paper has a whole page of personal ads for Valentine's Day," Joey said. "Listen to this."

" 'Wanted,' " Joey started reading. " 'Valentine dinner date with lady who doesn't mind a hamburger budget.' "

"Hamburgers by candlelight?" Aunt Becky poured syrup on Alex's pancakes and grinned at Uncle Jesse. "That sounds like one of our first dates."

Uncle Jesse frowned. "Hey! That was an original idea! Charming even."

"It was incredibly charming," Aunt Becky said.

"This one's even better!" Joey chuckled. "'Single female, five foot ten, looking for basketball player who likes cats and plays chess.'"

"I don't think she'll get any answers," D.J. said. "Basketball, cats, and chess? Doesn't sound like any guys I've ever met."

Stephanie didn't seem interested in the ads. "Aunt Becky," she interrupted. "I was wondering, do you still have the phone number for that juggler? The one you hired for the twins' last birthday party?"

Juggler! Michelle perked up. Aunt Becky's juggler was fantastic! Not only could Marvelous Manfred juggle bunches of weird stuff, he was funny, too. If Stephanie hired him, her class Valentine's Day party would be a smash success. This was completely awesome!

Aunt Becky nodded. "It's upstairs."

"You're not using him at the twins' pre-school Valentine's Day party, are you?" Stephanie smiled when Aunt Becky shook her head. "Good. I'll also need the name and number of your friend who does face painting."

Face painting, too! Michelle thought. *Whoa!* She was totally impressed. Stephanie was serious about making her class party the best there ever was. Rachel was going to faint from envy. Now she was more determined than ever to find Stephanie a date for the skating party.

And not just any boy will do, Michelle thought. *He has to be cute and fun and nice. He has to be the totally perfect valentine for Stephanie. I hope the perfect guy answers my ad soon.*

It was D.J.'s turn to do the dishes. As soon as everyone else left the kitchen, Michelle stuffed the classified section under her shirt and dashed upstairs. Since Stephanie was in their room, she ran into the bathroom and locked the door so no one would disturb her.

Will You Be My Valentine?

Michelle spread the paper on the floor. She'd noticed earlier that there was a column of ads in the personals section reserved entirely for kids. Most of them were from teenagers who were the same age as Stephanie. Michelle wanted to see how her ad stacked up against theirs.

Michelle read down the column. The more ads she read, the more she frowned. The teenage valentine ads were all clever or funny or distinctive in some way.

She recited her ad aloud from memory. "'Eighth-grade boy wanted for party date. Must know how to roller-skate.' "

Michelle sighed. Compared to the teenage ads in the *Chronicle,* her ad in the middle school newspaper seemed pretty vague and childish. Even the name she had attached to her e-mail address suddenly sounded lame. "Cupid Kid" was the first thing she had thought of when she placed the ad over the phone.

What if no cool boys e-mail me a response? Michelle worried.

She leaned back against the bathtub. That

was something she hadn't even considered. What if the only boys who wrote to her were total losers.

Or worse!

What if nobody *responds?*

Then Stephanie will be totally dateless, and it will be my *fault!*

STEPHANIE

Chapter
6

Monday afternoon Stephanie rushed out of her school as the final bell rang. She had to hurry if she was going to stop by Michelle's school to pick up the party fund on the way home.

Also, she couldn't wait to get out of her school building.

The past two days had been a nightmare.

Judy had gotten the gossip grapevine buzzing, just as Stephanie had feared. The rumor was that Sean broke off their Valentine's Day date because Stephanie planned to wear a Cupid costume to the party. Although nobody really seemed to believe it, the Cupid jokes had been flying since yesterday morning.

When Howie Atkins saw Stephanie coming toward him in the hall, he clutched his chest as though he had been shot. "I have been struck by an arrow of love," he cried as he staggered forward.

"Ha-ha, good one." Stephanie smiled with exaggerated sweetness as she walked by. If she let on how much the teasing hurt, Howie would just keep doing it.

Valerie Evans waved from farther down the hall. "Hey, Stephanie!"

"Hi, Val." Stephanie waved back. "What's up?"

"Not much." Valerie suppressed a giggle.

Naomi Ponti stepped out from behind Val. She placed the back of her hand against her forehead and swooned. "Oh, no! I'm in loooove."

Stephanie laughed and kept walking. She certainly didn't want anyone to think she was a poor sport. She had enough problems as it was.

Will You Be My Valentine?

She didn't know how long she could take this kind of treatment, though. Yesterday a seventh-grader had asked if she was wearing her diaper! Ugh! She wanted to crawl under a rock and hide until spring.

Stephanie sighed as she pushed through the school doors into the open air. There wasn't any point in trying to explain that the Cupid costume Judy had seen was for Ronny. Darcy and Allie had told everyone they knew that the rumor was false, but that news didn't seem to be traveling as fast as the rumor itself.

Everyone would probably be disappointed when Cupid Tanner didn't show up at the skating party. After all, Stephanie had to admit, it *was* a funny idea.

By the time Stephanie reached Michelle's school, she was smiling, which was good. She wanted to give Michelle's classmates the impression that she was happy and full of fun.

She especially had to impress that nasty Rachel.

The elementary school day ended later than that of the middle school, so all the kids were still seated when Stephanie entered Michelle's classroom. Sixteen pairs of fourth-grade eyes turned to stare. Mrs. Yoshida was collecting money in a basket.

Michelle waved from her desk.

The dark-haired girl sitting next to Michelle nudged her in the side. "Is that her?"

Rachel. Stephanie recognized the mean-spirited girl from the Harvest Festival. Michelle and their father had beaten out Rachel and her father in an apple pie-baking contest. That was probably one of the reasons Rachel liked to pick on Michelle so much.

"Yep." Michelle nodded. "That's my sister, Stephanie."

Rachel rolled her eyes and gave a huge sigh. "This party is going to be a disaster."

Michelle scowled. "No, it's not!"

Stephanie's temper flared, but she kept her anger in check. She gestured for Michelle to keep her cool, too. *The best way to make Rachel eat her words is to make sure the Valentine's Day party is a total hit*, Stephanie reminded herself.

"Hello, Stephanie!" Mrs. Yoshida smiled as she returned to her desk. "It's so nice of you to host the class Valentine's Day party for your sister."

"I'm really looking forward to it, Mrs. Yoshida. It'll be a *fantastic* party," Stephanie said with an emphatic nod. "Trust me."

"Yeah, right," Rachel muttered.

"You're just a kid," the boy sitting across from Rachel called out. "What do you know about giving parties?"

"Evan!" Mrs. Yoshida snapped. "Let's remember our manners."

Stephanie glanced at the teacher. "May I talk to the class?"

"Of course, dear." Mrs. Yoshida sat down. "The bell won't ring for a few minutes, and I have to count the money in the fund."

Okay, you're on! Stephanie thought. She took a deep breath and faced the class. All the kids were watching her.

"First of all, I'm not a kid. I'm a teenager," Stephanie corrected Evan. "And if there's one thing I know how to do, it's how to have fun!"

"Like throwing water balloons?" a boy with curly blond hair asked.

"Yeah!" Evan sounded skeptical. "Or playing tackle tag in the mud?"

"Not exactly, but my assistant"—Stephanie gestured toward Michelle—"and I have come up with some awesome ideas for your party on Friday."

When everyone turned to stare at Michelle, she stood up and took a quick bow.

"Oh, *that* makes me feel better." Rachel glared at Michelle, then turned her eyes on Stephanie. "Like what ideas?"

Stephanie gritted her teeth behind a tight smile. Now she really understood why Michelle had been so upset about Rachel giving her a hard time.

Rachel was good at giving people a hard time. Very good.

"Well, how about bakery cupcakes with gobs of pink and white icing." Stephanie wiggled her eyebrows and patted her stomach. "And a dynamite juggler who will do a show for all of you? He can juggle six things at once!"

"That's impossible." A girl with glasses and blond pigtails frowned at the boy beside her. "Isn't it, Jamar?"

"Nope." Jamar shook his head. "I saw this guy on TV do it."

Stephanie sensed that she was winning the class over, which boosted her own enthusiasm. "Not only that! Marvelous Manfred let's *you* pick the things he juggles! He'll juggle anything!"

"Can I ask him to juggle Mrs. Yoshida's desk?" Cassie, one of Michelle's best friends, grinned. Everyone but Rachel laughed.

"Well, I guess I should have said he'll juggle *almost* anything." Stephanie was surprised to find she was actually enjoying herself.

"Too bad." A boy sitting in the back grinned. "Desk juggling would have been cool!" Everybody laughed again.

"But why would this amazing juggler come to *our* party?" Rachel asked.

"Because I'm going to hire him," Stephanie said evenly. "In fact, I have an appointment with Mr. Manfred right after I leave here."

"She's getting a face painter, too," Michelle said for good measure.

"Cool!" The girl sitting in front of Michelle

clasped her hands. "Can the face painter do butterflies? I love butterflies."

"I'm not absolutely positive, but she probably can," Stephanie said. "I know she paints flowers and—"

The bell rang and all the kids jumped out of their seats.

Whew! I guess that's that! A wave of relief washed over Stephanie as the class stormed the cubbies to get their backpacks and jackets.

Michelle tapped Rachel on the shoulder and grinned when the girl looked back. "I told you my sister would be great, Rachel."

Considering Rachel's totally negative personality, Stephanie didn't blame Michelle for wanting to gloat a little. Especially now that the other kids were excited about the party.

"She hasn't *done* anything yet," Rachel pointed out.

"Just you wait, Rachel," Michelle said. "This is going to be the best party we ever had."

"I'll believe *that* when I see it," Rachel said.

"Here you are, Stephanie." Mrs. Yoshida walked over. She handed Stephanie an envelope and held out a pad. "This is all the money we've collected for the party. I just need you to sign this receipt."

"Okay." Stephanie took the pen from the teacher and signed on the dotted line.

"And don't forget to keep the receipts for what you spend," Mrs. Yoshida said. "Just bring them with you on Friday."

"Okay." Stephanie pointed to let Michelle know she would wait in the hall. "Thanks, Mrs. Yoshida. See you Friday."

Stephanie leaned against the wall outside the door and paused to take a deep breath. Fourth-graders were a tougher audience than she had remembered. Things would be a lot easier on her during the party, though. There would be three other people there to entertain the rowdy nine-year-olds. She'd just have to serve the refreshments and supervise.

Stephanie opened the envelope, hoping there was enough in the party fund to get plastic hearts she could fill with red and white jellybeans. She slowly counted the bills and gasped.

Sixty-two dollars and fifty cents!

That wasn't even close to being enough! There was no way she could get everything she had just promised on that kind of money.

The refreshments, favors, and craft supplies would cost thirty-five dollars and the costume rental was twenty-five. Aunt Becky had told her that Marvelous Manfred's fee was fifty dollars and her face painter friend charged twenty.

Stephanie needed *seventy* dollars more!

What was she going to do now?

MICHELLE

Chapter
7

Michelle rushed into the hall. "Stephanie! That was great!"

"Uh, yeah. Yeah, it was, wasn't it?" Stephanie was leaning against the wall with the party-fund envelope clutched in her hand. "All your friends are *really* looking forward to the party now, aren't they?"

"Boy, are they ever!" Michelle was so thrilled, she bounced as she talked. "Everybody's talking about it like it's a major event. Except Rachel."

"I'm not surprised." Stephanie sighed.

Michelle thought Stephanie looked a little

dazed, but that wasn't hard to understand. Dealing with Rachel *always* made her tired.

Michelle glanced at Stephanie's backpack. Hey, the special valentine edition of the John Muir Middle School newspaper was sticking out of the back pocket. Perfect!

"Are you going home now?" Michelle asked her sister.

"No." Stephanie straightened and put the envelope in her shoulder bag. "I've got to keep that appointment with Marvelous Manfred. And I'd better get going, or I'll be late."

"Okay, thanks for everything!" Michelle smiled at Stephanie and gave her a big hug. At the same time, she gently pulled the newspaper from Stephanie's backpack.

"No problem, Michelle," Stephanie said. She whirled around quickly.

Michelle giggled. Her sister didn't notice the newspaper that was now hidden behind Michelle's back. "See you later," she called.

Stephanie gave a groan and trudged down the hall. *What happened to change her good mood so fast?* Michelle wondered. Her sister wasn't nearly as enthusiastic about the appointment with the juggler as she had been a few minutes earlier.

Maybe she's nervous about meeting San Francisco's most famous party act, Michelle thought. But that didn't seem right. Stephanie never got anxious about meeting new people. *So what's the problem?*

"Here we are, Michelle," Cassie said.

Michelle looked up as Cassie and Mandy came out of the classroom.

"Are you ready to go?" Mandy asked.

"Yep." Michelle's mind drifted back into her own thoughts as she followed the two girls to the exit. She pushed through the doors.

Wait a minute! She knew why Stephanie looked so bummed. She was still upset because she didn't have a date for the skating party.

But that's going to change real fast. Michelle gripped the newspaper in her hand. That evening she was sure to have some e-mail responses on the computer. She just hoped Stephanie's perfect valentine date was among them.

Michelle crossed her fingers as she dashed to the sidewalk ahead of her friends.

When Michelle arrived home, she sat down for a minute on the front porch. She opened the middle school newspaper.

Her ad was buried in the middle of the personal ad page. She had to search the page three times before she found it.

Michelle sighed as she read the ad that came before hers. "'Seventh-grade guy looking for gorgeous girl who likes pizza, action-adventure movies, and video games.'" It wasn't as good as some of the ads in the Sunday *San Francisco Chronicle,* but it sounded more *teenage* than her ad.

Michelle moved on to the ad that came after hers. "'Lean and mean girl on track team seeks athletic boy who likes to dance." That ad sounded cooler than her ad, too.

"Hey, Michelle," a boy's voice called. "How are you doing?"

Michelle looked up to see the paperboy, Kevin, coming up the walk with the evening paper. "I'm not sure," she answered.

"Why not?" Kevin asked.

Michelle hesitated. Since Stephanie had told her to forget trying to find her a date for Valentine's Day, Michelle hadn't told *anyone* about her plan. Not even Cassie and Mandy. She didn't want anyone to accidentally let the secret slip.

Michelle was bursting to confide in someone. Since Kevin was really nice and didn't know Stephanie, what would be the harm in telling him?

"Can you keep a secret, Kevin?" Michelle asked.

Kevin raised his right hand. "Absolutely."

Michelle handed Kevin the middle school paper. She pointed to her ad. "Would you read that and tell me what you think?"

"Sure." Kevin tossed the evening paper on the porch and sat down to read Michelle's ad. He shrugged when he finished, but he didn't say anything.

"I knew it." Michelle groaned. "It's terrible, isn't it?"

"No, it's not terrible." Kevin frowned. "But it doesn't say much about the person who wants a party date. Except that she must be in eighth grade and likes to roller-skate."

"Oh." Michelle dropped her chin in her hands. "Then I probably won't get any e-mail responses."

"This is *your* ad?" Kevin sat back.

"Yes and no," Michelle said. "I put the ad in the school paper because I have to find Stephanie a date for her school skating party this Friday."

"Stephanie?" Kevin cocked his head.

"My sister," Michelle said. "The one in the eighth grade."

"Oh, yeah. The one with the blond hair and perky smile." Kevin nodded, then glanced at the school paper and frowned. "Do you really think you can find someone with an ad?"

Michelle shrugged. "Lots of people put personal ads in newspapers, so they must work."

"Maybe, but—" Kevin pushed on the brim of his baseball cap. He didn't look convinced.

"What?" Michelle asked. He obviously had something on his mind.

"Well, it just seems to me that Stephanie's perfect date should like some of the same things she does." Kevin shrugged. "You know, like music and TV shows. Plus, it might be hard to tell what a person's personality is like from an e-mail."

"Good point, Kevin. I'll think about that. After I see if anyone answers my ad." Michelle picked up Stephanie's backpack. "Thanks for the help."

"No problem." Kevin stood up.

"Bye!" Michelle called as the paperboy pedaled away.

After Kevin was gone, Michelle went into the living room. She could hear Joey whistling in the kitchen. The coast was clear. She tiptoed into the study and turned on the computer.

Michelle sat down and signed on to the Internet. She closed her eyes and listened until the modem static stopped. Then she opened one eye and punched in the password for Cupid Kid.

The *mail* signal flashed.

Someone had answered! Michelle gasped when she keyed the computer to deliver Cupid Kid's e-mail. Dozens of e-mail message titles began to appear!

I must have over a hundred answers! Michelle

realized. She couldn't possibly read all of them before Stephanie got back from the meeting with Marvelous Manfred, but she could read a few.

Michelle got a notebook and pencil from her backpack and settled in front of the computer. She clicked the mouse to open the first message. It was from a boy who was obviously too young for Stephanie.

"I'm not in 8th grade and I don't skate. But I like parties. Will they have cake and ice cream? Ted."

"I don't think so." Michelle deleted Ted's message and opened the second e-mail.

"Yo! Like I can dig the party on wheels, but you must be a total geek if you gotta advertise for a date! Spike."

"Definitely *not!*" Michelle hit Delete again. The third message wasn't much better.

"Hello. The only time I can get anyone to go

out with me is if it's a blind date. Does this count as a blind date? Milo."

Michelle didn't know why nobody wanted to date Milo, but that was all she needed to know to count him *out.* The next several e-mail responses were just as awful as the first three.

Discouraged, Michelle stared at the screen. Stephanie was putting one hundred percent into making her class Valentine's Day party great. Michelle had to find the perfect date for Stephanie's skating party. But if the rest of the responses were like these, she would be out of luck.

Maybe Kevin is right, Michelle thought. Stephanie's perfect Valentine's Day date had to be cute, cool, *and* like some of the same things she did.

How was she supposed to find someone like that?

Michelle didn't have a clue, and there were only three days left until Friday. Three days until the big party!

Chapter
8

Stephanie stared out the window of the city bus, deep in thought. *How am I going to deliver everything I promised to Michelle and the other kids on sixty-two dollars and fifty cents?*

She added up the party costs again. Again her calculations brought her to one unavoidable conclusion. She could buy the craft supplies, the cupcakes, candy and drinks, and the funny paper cups and have just enough left over to rent the Cupid costume. But it wouldn't be much of a Valentine's Day party without a juggler and a face painter.

Stephanie sighed. She had to figure out how

to do everything on a smaller budget. Michelle was counting on her to produce a wonderful party, and she just couldn't let her down.

When the bus reached Stephanie's stop, she got off filled with renewed determination. Michelle's class Valentine's Day party was going to be fantastic no matter *what* she had to do to make it that way.

Stephanie checked the address Aunt Becky had given her. Marvelous Manfred's combination office and studio was located in the middle of a quaint block of small specialty shops.

A bell jingled as Stephanie pushed through the door into a large room. The front section looked like a museum. Circus posters decorated the walls and glass display cases—filled with circus costumes and equipment—formed aisles. A counter with an old-fashioned cash register divided the front from the back half of the room. The rear half looked like a stage covered with exercise mats. Racks and tables of juggling supplies lined the wall on the right.

"Mr. Manfred?" Stephanie called.

Marvelous Manfred suddenly ran through a curtained doorway on the back wall and struck a performer's pose. Except for the padded slippers on his feet, he was wearing regular street clothes. However, he didn't walk to the counter where Stephanie waited. He did a series of impressive handsprings instead.

Stephanie's mouth fell open in astonishment. She gawked at the short, slim man a moment before she found her voice. "You're an acrobat, too?"

"When I have room. The average suburban house can rarely accommodate that particular talent." Manfred smiled. "How may I help you?"

Stephanie wondered if there was enough space in Michelle's classroom for an acrobatic demonstration. "I want to hire you for a kids' party."

"I see." Manfred pulled a large book from under the counter. "When and where?"

"Next Friday afternoon at my sister's school," Stephanie said. "At three-thirty."

"Hmmmm." Manfred flipped open the

book and ran his finger down one of the columns, checking his appearance dates.

Stephanie stared. It hadn't occurred to her that he might already be booked!

"You're in luck, I must say. I'm not busy at that time." Manfred smiled and bowed. A top hat appeared in his hand out of nowhere.

Stephanie's eyes widened. "I didn't know you did magic!"

"I don't!" Manfred scowled and tossed the hat in the air. He kept juggling it, tossing it from one hand to the other as he talked. "The pesky thing just keeps popping up whenever it feels like it. Now then—"

Whoa! Stephanie grinned. Marvelous Manfred was better than marvelous. He was amazing! Now if she could just get him to play Michelle's party without being paid right away, her worries would be over.

She decided to pay the man with her babysitting money. It would be worth it if it would make Michelle happy—and make Rachel shut up.

"What school is this?" A magic wand suddenly appeared in Manfred's hand. He began juggling it with the hat.

"Maybe we'd better discuss payment first," Stephanie said.

"Certainly. Twenty minutes. Fifty dollars."

"Okay. That sounds reasonable." Stephanie gave him her most charming smile. "Can I pay you on an installment plan? Say at five dollars a week?"

"Yes." Manfred nodded. "In which case I'll perform at your sister's school *ten* weeks from this Friday."

"But . . ." Stephanie stammered. "The party is *this* Friday, and there wasn't enough money in—"

"Fifty dollars. In advance." The man stopped juggling. He held up his hand and frowned. "No exceptions."

"But—this is an emergency!" Stephanie exclaimed. "My sister's reputation is on the line."

"I'm sorry." Manfred shrugged. "This is a business, you know. If I make one exception, I'll have to make another and another and pretty soon—poof! No more business."

"Yeah." Stephanie sighed and hung her head. "I understand. It's just that—"

"Don't despair, fair maid!" Manfred handed Stephanie a plain business card with a name and address. "This gentleman has an office right around the corner. He's a bit new at the trade, and considering the competition"— the juggler swept into a humble bow—"he might consider being paid in weekly installments."

"Ummm, thanks." Disappointed but grateful, Stephanie left the juggler's studio and hurried down the street.

The Amazing Archibald's office wasn't nearly as impressive as Marvelous Manfred's, but Stephanie was desperate. She walked inside and interrupted a tall, thin man juggling four colorful balls. He was wearing a green suit and white hightops. His pants were too short and the jacket was too tight. His bright red tie clashed horribly!

"Are you Archibald?" Stephanie asked.

The man jumped and fumbled all the balls. One ball hit him in the chin when it bounced off the floor. He adjusted his wire-rimmed glasses. "Yes. Are you in the habit of disturbing people when they're practicing?"

"No." Stephanie frowned. "But I can leave if you don't want the job."

"Job?" Archibald's eyes lit up and he rubbed his hands together. "When and where?"

"At a fourth-grade school party next Friday afternoon," Stephanie said. "Are you already booked?"

"I don't think so." Archibald glanced around the small, cluttered room. "I seem to have misplaced my appointment book, but I'll remember. How much does this gig pay?"

"Not so fast." Stephanie realized Archibald was a little *too* eager to find work. She could probably hire him for half of Manfred's fee. Even so, the money was coming out of *her* pocket. "I'd like an audition first. If you don't mind."

"Mind? No, of course not! Why should I mind?" The man seemed nervous as he gathered the four balls from around the room. "Watch this."

Stephanie watched as Archibald got all four

balls moving, then winced when he dropped one.

"Slippery little guys, aren't they?" Archibald grinned. "That was a joke. It's part of my act."

Sure it is. Stephanie's eyes narrowed. "Can you juggle anything else?"

"Oh, yes." Archibald turned to look at her and dropped the other balls. "Lots of things. Apples and oranges are my specialty."

"Really." Stephanie just nodded. With a little practice, *she* could probably juggle four apples! *Wait a minute, that isn't a bad idea!* she thought.

Stephanie reviewed her options. Unfortunately, she couldn't afford Marvelous Manfred. The Amazing Archibald would be cheaper, but he was a lousy juggler who told rotten jokes and dressed terribly. Plus, since he couldn't find his appointment book, she couldn't shake the feeling that he'd forget to show up.

Which leaves only one option.

She'd just have to learn to juggle and hope she didn't make a total fool of herself in front of Michelle's class!

"Would you show *me* how to juggle, Mr. Archibald?" Stephanie reached into her shoulder bag and pulled out a five-dollar bill.

The juggler grabbed the bill from her hand. "Five dollars buys you a ten-minute lesson."

"Works for me!"

Ten minutes later Stephanie left the office feeling more depressed than ever. Juggling was a lot harder than it looked. She could barely manage to keep *two* balls moving for a few seconds before she dropped them.

Stephanie was sure she'd get better at juggling with practice. But what if Rachel—and the rest of Michelle's class—wouldn't be satisfied with anyone but Marvelous Manfred?

MICHELLE

Chapter
9

"Where do you want to meet up later?" Michelle asked.

Aunt Becky had taken Stephanie, Michelle, Cassie, and Mandy to the mall with her. Stephanie was there to buy valentine party supplies, Michelle knew. But Michelle was there for an even more important purpose.

Aunt Becky straightened her purse on her shoulder. "Why don't you girls meet here at the fountain in an hour," she suggested. "I'll bring the car around to those doors straight ahead. You can meet me there."

"Okay," Stephanie agreed.

"If anyone needs me, I'll be in the Kids Barn, getting clothes for the twins," Aunt Becky informed them. "See you all in an hour." She walked off toward the Kids Barn.

"Where are you guys going?" Stephanie asked before Michelle had a chance to take a step.

"We've got some things to do," Michelle said. "For Valentine's Day. Right?"

She nudged Cassie and Mandy. She had finally told them that she was looking for a date for Stephanie. She also told them that they shouldn't say a word about her plan to Stephanie.

"Right." Cassie and Mandy both nodded.

"Oh!" Stephanie grinned. "Do you want to look for valentines to give the kids in your class?"

"Ummm—I want to look for valentines— yeah." Michelle grinned, too. *But* not *to give my class!* she thought.

"Well, I guess that would be okay." Stephanie glanced around. The mall wasn't too busy for a Wednesday afternoon, and most of the people wandering around were kids.

Will You Be My Valentine?

"Meet you here in an hour, Steph." Michelle walked off with Cassie and Mandy.

The night before, she had read all the e-mail responses to her ad and had come up with a big, fat zero! That's when she decided to take Kevin's advice.

She was determined to find Stephanie's date here at the mall instead of through e-mail. She just had to think of a way to figure out which boys shared Stephanie's interests.

Michelle's spirits soared when she walked into the CD store. The place was *full* of kids, just as she suspected.

"Okay, Michelle," Mandy said. "What's your plan?"

"Well, first I'm going to go say hi to Mr. Porter, the manager." Michelle pointed to the middle-aged man behind the counter. "He's a friend of my dad's."

"Then what?" Cassie looked around. "There are a lot of cute guys here who are Stephanie's age!"

Michelle thought for a moment. "Stephanie's favorite group right now is Cellar Blue," she said. "Maybe I could hang around the display that has their latest CD and see who shows up. That way, I'll know Stephanie and the boys I meet will have something in common—music!"

"Good idea." Mandy frowned. "What do you want us to do?"

"Well, let's see . . . you could wander around the store and spot anyone Stephanie might like!"

"Okay. We can do that." Cassie nodded. "Come on, Mandy."

After Michelle spoke to Mr. Porter, she stationed herself near the display of Cellar Blue's latest album. She pretended to read the back of a CD while she kept an eye out for a likely prospect.

At first, the only kids who showed any interest in Cellar Blue were girls! Then, finally, a boy with sandy-colored hair stopped by the display. He was the same height as Stephanie and wore baggy pants with a black designer-logo T-shirt. Michelle thought he was pretty handsome.

So far so good, she thought.

Michelle put down the CD she was holding

and strolled over to the Cellar Blue display. The boy stared at the CD in his hand and frowned as though he wasn't sure he wanted to buy it. Michelle seized the opening.

"That's a super album," Michelle said.

"Is it?" The boy smiled at Michelle. "How old are you?"

"I'm nine, but my *really* pretty sister, who has a *terrific* personality, is *thirteen*, and she just loves it!" Michelle tensed, waiting for a reaction. She wanted the boy to ask more about Stephanie.

"Thirteen?" the boy asked. "So someone who's fourteen would probably like this, right?" He held up the CD.

Michelle nodded. Excellent! This guy was fourteen, and *exactly* the kind of date she was hoping to find for Stephanie! He was good-looking, nice, and just the right age and everything!

"Do you like to roller-skate?" Michelle *had* to ask. A date who didn't roller-skate wouldn't be much fun at a roller-skating party.

"I used to." The boy laughed. "Being a senior in high school doesn't leave much time for things like that, though. I'm too busy applying to colleges and stuff."

"You're fourteen and a senior in high school?" Michelle asked, puzzled. "You must be a genius!"

"Well, I'm not exactly a genius. And I'm not fourteen—I'm eighteen. I understand why you'd get confused, though. I'm kind of short."

"Oh," Michelle groaned.

"Well, thanks for the advice on this," the boy said. "My cousin's fourteenth birthday is tomorrow and I didn't have a clue what to get her." He walked toward the cashier.

"You're welcome," Michelle called after him. Stunned, she went back to her lookout position. Eighteen was way too old for Stephanie.

Michelle decided she'd have to find out boys' ages *before* she considered asking them to be Stephanie's valentine.

Within a few minutes another boy was browsing the Cellar Blue rack. She sized him up as he read the back of the album. He had reddish-brown hair cut in the latest style, and freckles. He wore jeans and an unbuttoned shirt over a T-shirt. That was cool. Michelle decided to talk to him.

"Excuse me, but there's something I *really* have to know." Although he didn't *look* older than fourteen, Michelle wasn't taking any chances. "How old are you?"

The boy scowled. "Why should I tell you, twerp!"

Twerp?

Michelle bristled but gave him another chance. Her question *had* been a little bold. "Well, do you like blond girls who have a great sense of humor and like Cellar Blue and want to go roller-skating?"

"I don't want to go roller-skating with *you*. You're just a kid. Now do me a favor and leave me alone." Shaking his head, the boy shoved the CD back in the rack and stomped away.

"Fine, I will!" Furious *and* frustrated, Michelle leaned on the rack and sighed. That boy hadn't even given her a chance to explain herself. *And* he was majorly grumpy. "This is *not* going like I thought it would," she said to herself.

"Hey! Are you okay?" another boy asked.

Michelle's breath caught in her throat when she looked up. *Wow!* The boy looking down at her was tall with blond hair—and he was gorgeous!

"You look kind of worried. Are you lost or something?" the boy asked, concerned.

"No, I'm not lost." Michelle answered. "Are you fourteen?"

The boy jerked back, surprised by the blunt question. "Uh—almost. Why?"

"What's your name?" Michelle pressed on. "Do you like Cellar Blue?"

"Jeff. And Cellar Blue's okay." The boy shrugged. "Why?"

Astounded by her luck, Michelle plunged ahead. "Because I have to find a Valentine's Day date for—"

"Jeff! I found it!" A girl with long red hair and blue eyes came toward the boy, waving a CD. Her eyes narrowed when she noticed Michelle. "Who's the little flirt?"

Michelle's heart sank when the girl hooked

her arm through Jeff's. She was obviously Jeff's girlfriend.

"She needs a Valentine's Day date," Jeff said. "Isn't that sweet?" He smiled at Michelle.

"Aren't you kind of young to be dating?" the girl asked Michelle in a condescending tone.

"I'm not looking for *me*," Michelle snapped. The girl's nasty attitude was totally annoying. "I'm looking for a date for my sister!"

"Oh, well. I don't think you'll find one here." The girl rolled her eyes at Jeff. "Come on, Jeff. We've got a lot to do."

"Okay." Jeff waved at Michelle as he walked away.

Figures, Michelle thought. *I find two great guys for Stephanie and one's too old and the other one already has a girlfriend!*

Michelle glanced at the clock above the checkout counter. She had only thirty minutes left before she had to meet Stephanie. And she'd talked to only two people so far!

Hmmm, maybe it was time to try something different. The question was *what?* Maybe one of her friends had an idea.

Michelle found Cassie and Mandy poring through the discount CD bin. "This isn't working. Can either of you think of somewhere else to look for Stephanie's perfect valentine?"

"I don't know, but I'm hungry. Let's get something to eat!" Cassie suggested.

"Good idea," Mandy said. "What do you want?"

"Ice cream!" Michelle grinned. "And while we're eating, we can look for someone who orders Stephanie's favorite flavor!"

"What *is* Stephanie's favorite flavor?" Mandy asked.

"Chocolate fudge explosion," Michelle said.

The girls hurried to the ice-cream shop. Michelle ordered a two-scoop hot fudge sundae with three spoons and sat at a table near the counter with her friends. In the fifteen minutes it took them to finish their ice cream, only two boys ordered chocolate fudge explosion.

Both of them were about six years old.

Out of time and ideas, the three friends left the ice-cream shop to meet Stephanie. They detoured into the card shop and picked out packs of valentines so Stephanie wouldn't be suspicious when they returned empty-handed.

Michelle shuffled toward the center of the mall with Cassie and Mandy. She couldn't believe she had struck out again. She *still* hadn't found Stephanie a valentine. Maybe, if she was lucky, she'd have some *new* e-mail replies to her ad today! And maybe she'd find *one* dynamite response. *That's all I need,* she told herself. *One.*

Stephanie was waiting when Michelle and her friends arrived. The Cupid costume was slung over her shoulder, and she was loaded down with shopping bags. "Let's go, guys," she called. "I want to be waiting outside when Aunt Becky pulls up. Did you get your valentines?"

Cassie and Mandy nodded.

"Yeah." Michelle held up her bag. *Even though they aren't the kind of valentine I was looking for,* she thought. "I can carry some of those bags if you want," she offered her sister.

"Thanks." Stephanie set the bags on the floor and handed the smallest bags to

Michelle. She rearranged the Cupid costume over her arm. She looked toward the far side of the mall—and frowned.

Michelle followed her gaze—and gasped. The couple from the CD store walked by—Jeff and his snotty girlfriend. Jeff didn't notice them, but the girl pointed at Stephanie and waved.

"You—you know her?" Michelle stuttered.

"Yes, and she's making my life miserable," Stephanie groaned.

Michelle's eyes widened. "She is?"

"Unfortunately." Stephanie picked up the remaining bags.

"How is she making your life miserable?" Cassie asked.

Stephanie shook her head. "Judy's a big gossip—a total blabbermouth. She saw me in the costume shop the other day looking for this Cupid costume. After that she told everyone at school that I was going to the skating party dressed as Cupid!"

Stephanie sighed. "And now here I am with the costume in my hands. The rumors will probably start all over again."

Michelle gulped. She had a feeling that the Cupid-costume gossip was the least of Stephanie's worries.

"Uh-oh." Mandy winced. "Here she comes!"

Michelle froze.

Judy stopped in front of the group. "I see you picked up your Cupid costume, Stephanie. I can't wait to see you wearing it!"

Stephanie's cheeks turned red with embarrassment. "I told you that this costume isn't for me, Judy. It's for my sister's class party, and someone else is wearing it."

"Uh-huh." Judy looked at Michelle. "Is *this* your sister?"

"Yes." Stephanie frowned. "Why?"

Judy laughed out loud. "No reason. See ya!" She giggled again as she walked away.

Stephanie sighed. "Come on. Let's get out of here."

Michelle just nodded. She didn't want to tell Stephanie what had happened at the CD store.

Maybe Judy *was* laughing at the Cupid costume. But chances were Judy was laughing for another reason. Because she knew

Stephanie's younger sister was trying to find her a date.

Maybe she won't tell anyone, Michelle reasoned. *But what if she does?*

Then there was only *one* thing that would help Stephanie. She would have to show up at the skating party with a totally nice, completely great-looking boy!

That wasn't going to happen unless Michelle found the right boy, soon!

STEPHANIE

Chapter 10

Stephanie popped another chip in her mouth and allowed herself to relax. It was lunchtime on Thursday, and she hadn't been the target of a single Cupid joke all morning.

Maybe everyone's starting to realize I'm the innocent victim of Judy's malicious gossip, she reasoned.

"The skating party isn't going to be as much fun if you're not there, Stephanie." Allie pushed her macaroni and cheese around her plate.

"Ditto that." Darcy sat with her chin propped in one hand sipping milk through a straw. "You could come *without* a date, you know. It's not like you'd be completely alone."

"Right." Allie nodded. "We'll be there."

"With Chris and Rusty," Stephanie said. "You know, normally I wouldn't care if I had a date or not, but this is the *Valentine's* Day party. I mean, I've put up with enough ridicule this week, don't you think? Can you imagine what Judy would do if I showed up alone?"

Allie nodded. "No doubt about it. That girl is *bad* news."

"Stephanie!" Lucy Johnson rushed up to the table with Katherine Armor. "Just the person we wanted to see."

Stephanie tensed, waiting for one of the girls to ask how she prevented diaper rash or something else equally lame.

"We heard you lost your job," Katherine said.

"What job?" Stephanie asked.

"As Cupid!" Lucy grinned.

"Yeah," Katherine said. "We heard your little sister took over. Do you think she could find us Valentine's Day dates, too?"

Both girls laughed, then walked away.

Darcy stared after them. She turned to Stephanie. "What was that all about?"

"Sounds like another vicious rumor." Allie's eyes flashed.

"Judy again?" Darcy asked.

"Who else?" Stephanie frowned. *But how did Judy find out that Michelle wanted to look for a date for me?* she wondered.

"Stephanie!" Roberta Edgars rushed over. "Could I have your sister's phone number? I need a date for next Halloween."

"Very funny, Roberta." Stephanie scowled. She had had enough of this harassment. "So funny I forgot to laugh."

"Well!" Roberta huffed. "I guess some people can't take a joke!"

"What is everyone talking about?" Darcy asked. "What do they mean about your sister finding you a date?"

Stephanie wasn't sure, but she had a good idea. And she intended to ask Michelle about it as soon as she got home!

Stephanie was waiting in their room when Michelle entered after school. "Okay, Michelle," she started right in. "What have you been up to behind my back?"

"Up to?" Michelle stopped and blinked. Stephanie recognized her "innocent" look.

She took a deep breath. *Michelle was just trying to help,* she reminded herself. *I shouldn't be so hard on her.*

"I am not mad," Stephanie coached herself out loud.

"Good!" Michelle tossed her backpack on her bed and turned to leave.

"Halt!" Stephanie stood up and pointed to a chair. "I'm not mad, but I do want an explanation."

Michelle sat down and stared at the floor.

"There was a rumor flying around school today that you were trying to find me a date. How did that rumor get started?" Stephanie asked.

"Well, it might have been Judy," Michelle muttered. "That snotty girl we ran into at the mall."

"And why would Judy Morton think you were trying to find a date for me?" Stephanie asked.

Michelle winced. "Jeff probably told her I was."

"Jeff!" Stephanie squealed. "Jeff Perdue? How would *he* know anything about this?"

"Well, I told him." Michelle shrugged. "Sort of."

"How do you sort-of tell someone something, Michelle?" Stephanie managed to stay calm, but it wasn't easy. "Explain the whole story. Now."

Michelle gulped. "Well, I told Jeff I was looking for a date when I spotted him in the CD store—"

Stephanie gasped. "You were scouting for dates for me in the CD store?"

"Right, and Jeff thought I meant I needed a date for *me*," Michelle continued. "But when Judy said something nasty about me being too young to date, I got mad and told her it wasn't for me, it was for my sister. Only she didn't know *you* were my sister. . . ."

"Until she saw us leaving the mall together," Stephanie finished Michelle's sentence. She sank onto the edge of her bed. "Ugh!" she groaned.

"I'm really sorry, Stephanie," Michelle said. "I didn't mean to make trouble for you."

"I know. You were just trying to be nice."

Stephanie rubbed her face with her hands. *Things aren't as bad as they sound,* she told herself.

"Just do me a favor, okay? Please, *please* stop going around town trying to find me a date! It looks pathetic. And I need to be able to tell my friends that the rumor *honestly* isn't true. Understand?"

Michelle paused. "Okay. I promise to stop going around town looking for a date for you."

"Thank you." Stephanie fell backward onto her bed.

Michelle stared down at her. "I thought you were going to Darcy's house to make valentines for the class party."

"I am. Right after I make a phone call."

"When is that?" Michelle asked.

"As soon as I recover from shock." Stephanie sat up. Michelle was still staring at her. "In a minute, okay?"

"Okay." Michelle hesitated for a moment, then left.

Stephanie shook her head, gave one last groan of frustration, and immediately threw herself into the party preparations. She couldn't do anything about the "date" rumor until the next day, anyway, she reasoned.

Stephanie got the face painter's telephone number from Aunt Becky. She went to the kitchen phone and dialed. She had been trying to reach Cecilia Conrad all week, but she hadn't returned her calls. This time she answered the phone.

"Ms. Conrad! I'm so glad I finally reached you. This is Stephanie Tanner, Becky's niece?"

"Oh, yes!" Ms. Conrad seemed happy to hear from her. "What can I do for you, Stephanie?"

"Well," Stephanie began, "I want to hire you to do some face painting at my sister's class Valentine's Day party after school this Friday. I was wondering if I could pay you in installments. Say, five dollars a week?"

"This Friday?" Ms. Conrad asked. "I'm so sorry, Stephanie, but I'm working another party Friday afternoon."

"You are? Oh. Well, thank you anyway." Stephanie hung up the phone and collapsed on a kitchen chair.

Everything she planned for Michelle's party was falling apart! She had spent hours practicing juggling in the garage the night before. The best she had managed was keeping three tennis balls going for nine point five seconds. Now she didn't even have the face painter for the party!

"Okay," Stephanie muttered to herself. "Time for Plan B. How hard can face painting be?"

"Actually, roses are pretty difficult to paint." Aunt Becky walked in the back door with the twins.

"Hi, Steph!" Nicky grinned.

"I'm hungry." Alex climbed onto a chair.

"Hi, guys." Stephanie turned back to Becky and explained her problem.

"Maybe I can help, Stephanie," Becky said. "If you're going to paint faces yourself, I'll call Cecilia to find out what you need. I'll make sure I pick all that stuff up for you."

"Thanks, Aunt Becky. I really appreciate it,

but I won't be able to pay you back right away."

"Don't worry about that!" Becky grinned as she herded the twins up the stairs. "You can pay me back in babysitting time."

"That's a deal!" Stephanie glanced at the clock and ran back upstairs to get her craft supplies and tennis balls. She was headed to Darcy's for a little while.

If Darcy and Allie didn't mind making valentines, Stephanie could get in some more juggling practice. Face painting would be a snap by comparison as long as the kids were happy with fancy stars and daisies.

Stephanie threw her supplies into a backpack, then headed out the door. She was halfway outside when the phone rang.

"Hello?" Stephanie answered.

"Hi, Stephanie," Ronny Harkin said from the other end of the line. "I hate to tell you this, but I have bad news. I forgot I have a dentist appointment tomorrow and my mom won't let me cancel. I can't play Cupid at your sister's class party. I'm really sorry."

"Ummm, no problem, Ronny," Stephanie responded. "Bye."

Stephanie was numb when she hung up. Not only was she the juggler and the face painter for Michelle's party, now she had to be Cupid, too!

Can I really do everything, she wondered, *and still pull off a fantastic party for Michelle?*

MICHELLE

Chapter 11

Michelle went downstairs and turned on the TV. She was eager to check Cupid Kid's e-mail, but she didn't want Stephanie to see her at the computer.

She wished Stephanie would hurry up and leave for Darcy's!

Michelle sat on the couch and laid her head on the armrest. She had read and saved a few new answers to her ad yesterday after she got back from the mall. But she hadn't found a *perfect* reply.

"I'm leaving now, Michelle." Stephanie stopped at the bottom of the stairs. Her backpack was stuffed full of valentine supplies. "Don't forget your promise."

"I won't."

Michelle smiled to herself. She had promised not to look for Stephanie's date around *town*! And she wouldn't. She would look for him on the Internet. That wasn't the same thing.

Michelle waited a whole minute after Stephanie left the house. Then she rushed to the computer and signed on to the Internet. *Oh, no.* Michelle's heart sank. Cupid Kid had no mail.

Now what? she wondered. She turned off the computer and went out to the porch. She sat on the steps to think. She had tried everything to find Stephanie a date for the skating party, but she had failed!

She felt terrible, but she couldn't think of anything else to do. It seemed as if her mission to find Stephanie the perfect date was at an end.

"Hi, Michelle!" Kevin parked his bike and came up the walk with the newspaper. "How's everything today?"

Will You Be My Valentine?

Michelle sighed. "Not very good. I totally struck out trying to find Stephanie the perfect valentine date for her skating party."

Kevin sat down beside her. "That's too bad, but I'm sure you tried your best."

"Yeah." Michelle sighed. "But I feel just awful about it. Stephanie's hosting my class Valentine's Day party tomorrow because nobody else could do it. She's worked so hard to help me, and now I've totally let her down."

"Maybe there's something you haven't thought of," Kevin said. "Or someone?"

"I don't think so." Michelle shook her head. "I even took *your* advice and went to the mall to find somebody who likes Cellar Blue. That was a total waste of time. I couldn't find anyone who was right for Stephanie."

"I like Cellar Blue," Kevin said.

Michelle sat up with a start. She turned slowly to look at the paperboy. Kevin adjusted the brim of his baseball cap and smiled. His brown eyes twinkled.

Why haven't I ever noticed how cute Kevin is? Michelle stared in disbelief. *Duh! Because he's the paperboy and I never paid attention before!*

"I like all kinds of music, actually," Kevin said, "but alternative is my favorite."

Michelle felt a rush of happiness. Kevin was nice, and sweet, and cute, and . . .

Could he be the perfect valentine date for Stephanie!

Michelle hesitated. She was almost afraid to ask Kevin any questions. *What if I get the wrong answers?* she thought. But she had to be one hundred percent sure about Kevin for Stephanie's special date.

"How old are you?" Michelle leaned forward.

"Thirteen," Kevin answered.

Michelle swallowed hard. He was the right age.

"Do you like going to the roller rink?" she asked.

"I *love* going to the roller rink." Kevin grinned. "I got my first pair of clip-on skates for my sixth birthday. I went around with skinned elbows and knees for weeks! My mom says she spent a fortune on bandages."

Michelle laughed. Kevin didn't have a problem carrying on a conversation, either. That was a definite plus for a Valentine's Day date.

Stephanie talked—a lot! And Kevin was funny, too!

"Do you like chocolate ice cream?"

"Not really." Kevin wrinkled his nose. "I know that's weird for a kid, but my favorite flavor is butter pecan. With hot fudge."

Did favorite ice cream flavors really matter? Michelle wondered for two seconds. *Probably not.*

Michelle tensed as she asked the most important question of all. "You probably already have a date for the school skating party, don't you?"

"Well," Kevin explained. "I go to school in a different district than you guys. We're not having a skating party. So I guess the answer is no."

"Really? That's great!" There was one more question left. A question that Michelle hadn't asked anyone. Nobody else had been this perfect for Stephanie.

"I don't suppose you'd want to be Stephanie's date, would you, Kevin?"

"I'd love to!" Kevin's smile got wider. "Except I've never actually *met* Stephanie. I mean, I've seen her, but she's never really *said* anything to me."

"No problem!" Michelle giggled with excitement. "You can meet her tomorrow at my school. Get there right before my class party ends at four o'clock, then I can introduce you to Stephanie. You can go to the roller rink from there!"

After Michelle gave Kevin the directions to her school, he handed her the newspaper and got up to leave.

"I'm really glad you picked me to take Stephanie to the skating party, Michelle. I'm flattered. Thanks." Kevin grinned from ear to ear as he ran back to his bike.

Michelle jumped up and down as Kevin rode away. "Yes! I did it! I found Stephanie's perfect valentine!"

Now I just hope Stephanie likes him.

STEPHANIE

Chapter
12

Oh, no! There go the cupcakes!" Stephanie winced as her stack of party stuff tilted.

Darcy jumped forward and stopped the cupcake box from falling. "Got it."

"That was close." Allie sagged under the weight of two grocery bags. One was full of candy, canned drinks, and whipped cream. The other held Stephanie's homemade valentines, face-painting kit, costume accessories, and tennis balls.

"Thanks, Darce." Stephanie held the elementary school door open with her foot. After Darcy and Allie were inside, she let the door close behind her. She led the way to the rest room that was right down the hall from Michelle's class. She planned to use it as a base of operations because she didn't want the kids to see the Cupid costume before she made her big entrance in it.

"I don't know how I would have gotten all this stuff over here without you guys." Stephanie had forgotten that everyone in her family was busy today. Allie's mom had saved the day and driven the three girls to Michelle's school. "Thanks."

"No problem." Darcy dropped her bags on the sink counter.

Allie put down her pile, then took the cupcake box off the top and set it aside. "I still wish you'd change your mind about coming to the skating party, though."

"No way." Stephanie shook her head as she pulled a tray out of her bag and started separating the cartoon paper cups. "I'm not going to make my ruined social standing worse by showing up at the roller rink alone."

"Can't say that I blame you. I'm sorry, Steph. Everything will straighten out in a day or two. You'll see. Judy will have someone else to pick on by then." Allie looked at her watch. She frowned. "Guess we'd better get going." ←

"Have fun. And that's an order!" Stephanie smiled and waved as her friends left the rest room. Then she turned and finished setting up the refreshment trays. She put the tray arranged with cups full of candy on top of the cupcake box. Then she picked both of them up and headed for Michelle's classroom.

Stephanie paused in the hall outside the door. Mrs. Yoshida was handing out bags the class had decorated for Valentine's Day. She turned and caught sight of Stephanie. Mrs. Yoshida gave her an encouraging nod. Stephanie took a deep breath. *Well, here goes nothing.*

Stephanie stepped through the door. "Ta-*dah*! It's party time!" she announced.

Michelle gave Stephanie two thumbs-ups. Her smile was so big, her whole face shone.

All the kids except Rachel cheered and applauded as Stephanie swept to the far side of the room. She left the cupcake box on one of the round activity tables and distributed the paper cups full of candy. Giggles and laughs erupted as the kids read the funny sayings on the cups.

Those are a big winner, Stephanie thought. *Maybe I can pull this party off after all!* She sure hoped so—for Michelle's sake.

"All right, class!" Mrs. Yoshida clapped her hands for attention. "While Stephanie passes out the rest of the refreshments, you can pass out your valentines. In an orderly manner, please!"

Stephanie hurried back to the rest room and returned with a tray of clear plastic cups. They were filled with fruit punch and topped with a dab of whipped cream.

"Whoa!" Jamar took a sip and grinned. "This tastes great!"

"It looks just like a valentine's drink should look," Cassie said. "Red and white. Cool!"

So far so good! Stephanie started to relax as she set a cupcake on everyone's desk. She served Michelle's table last. Michelle and Erin were showing their valentines to each other. Their bags were full of cards.

"Love, José." Erin blushed crimson and covered her face with her hands.

"Ooooh, Erin." Michelle giggled, then looked up when Stephanie set a cupcake in front of her. "Everyone *loves* snacks!"

"Refreshments are easy," Rachel said. "Where's this awesome juggler?"

Stephanie noticed that Rachel had only a few valentines in her pile. She hadn't opened any of them. "The juggler will be here in a few minutes. After I'm done face painting."

"Huh?" Michelle's mouth fell open.

"After *you're* done?" Rachel threw up her hands. "*This* should be good," she said.

Stephanie leaned over and whispered to Michelle. "Sorry. Aunt Becky's friend was busy. I didn't have any choice."

"That's okay," Michelle whispered back, then smiled. "I'm sure you'll do just fine. How hard can it be?"

Stephanie wondered the same thing as she carried the empty trays back to the rest room. She filled a cup with water and grabbed her hand mirror. Then she took the old face-painting kit Cecilia had given Aunt Becky back to the classroom and set up at the round activity table.

"Who's first?" Stephanie asked.

Michelle looked around and raised her hand when no one else volunteered. Then the girl who liked butterflies jumped out of her seat.

"Me! I want to go first! Please!"

"Calm down, Denise!" Mrs. Yoshida smiled.

Stephanie paled. She couldn't pick Michelle because it would look like she was favoring her sister. "Does it have to be a butterfly, Denise? How about a star or a daisy?"

Denise shook her head. "I want a butterfly."

While Stephanie attempted to create a blue butterfly with red highlights on Denise's cheek, the rest of the kids finished exchanging their valentines and eating their snacks.

Face painting wasn't as easy as Stephanie had thought it would be. She looked at the finished butterfly in dismay. The colors had run together and turned muddy!

"Let me see!" Denise picked up the mirror.

Rachel stepped up behind Stephanie, then

walked away in disgust. "That butterfly looks like a *bat*."

Mandy came over and cocked her head. "Or an ink splatter."

Denise put down the mirror and looked at Stephanie. "Does this paint wash off with water?"

So much for face painting! Then Stephanie had an idea.

"Mandy!" Stephanie stood up. "Why don't you try this? I bet you can paint something totally cool! And when you're done, someone else can take a turn. You can all paint each other's faces."

"Wow! That might be fun!" Grinning, Mandy sat down and waved to Cassie. "Come on, Cassie! I need a victim."

"You can do my other cheek, too!" Denise turned her head.

While Mrs. Yoshida collected empty cups and cupcake wrappers in a trash bag, Stephanie ran back to the rest room. She put on a tall green St. Patrick's Day hat Joey had lent her and slipped on the red suit jacket Aunt Becky had let her borrow. She put two tennis balls under the hat and stuffed one in each of the jacket pockets. Clutching a glittering magic wand D.J. had used last Halloween, she hurried back to the classroom.

Stephanie paused outside the door to take a deep breath. Then she shouted, "Let's hear a big round of applause for—"

Stephanie jumped through the door and struck a pose like Marvelous Manfred.

"The Stupendous Stephanie!"

Stunned silence filled the room.

"I knew it!" Rachel smiled. "Michelle's sister is a cheat! She promised us Marvelous Manfred!"

"That's enough, Rachel!" Mrs. Yoshida said.

"Uh, Marvelous Manfred couldn't make it." Stephanie shrugged when she caught Michelle's eye.

Michelle started clapping her hands. "Woo-hoo, Stephanie!"

A few of the other kids joined in.

Encouraged by Michelle and her friends' support, Stephanie sprang into her act. "The Stupendous Stephanie is not *just* a juggler. No! She's got a few surprises up her sleeve, too." Stephanie made a show of looking up her sleeve, then frowned. "But I think they skipped school today!"

Scattered giggles rippled through the room.

"No, wait!" Stephanie rolled her eyes up toward the green hat perched on her head. "I bet they're hiding under my hat!"

"This is *so* lame," Rachel said loudly.

Stephanie ignored her. Moving like she was afraid of what she might find, she pushed on the brim of the hat with the wand. The hat toppled backward off her head and the tennis balls fell on the floor and bounced. Stephanie grabbed them before they rolled between the desks. "Ah-ha!"

"What's the surprise?" Evan asked.

Stephanie blinked. "The tennis balls under my hat."

"Oh."

Oh, boy. *That was* so *lame,* Stephanie thought. She began to juggle the two tennis balls before she lost her audience. Miraculously, she kept the two balls moving between her hands without dropping them. The only problem was that she really had to concentrate, so she couldn't talk and juggle at the same time.

"Can't you even juggle three?" another boy called out.

Stephanie nodded and braced herself. Keeping her eyes on the moving tennis balls, she reached into her pocket for a third ball.

Oh, no! Stephanie tugged at the ball. *It's jammed! I can't get it out!* The two balls she was already juggling dropped to the floor. Stephanie caught them as they bounced. She struck another pose.

"Ta-*daaaaah!*" she yelled.

The kids just stared at her.

Michelle motioned for her to keep going.

"Tennis balls are such slippery little guys." Stephanie looked at Evan and tossed the ball. "Catch!"

Evan was surprised, but he caught the tennis ball.

Stephanie held out her hand and Evan tossed the ball back. "Maybe you should take up juggling!" Stephanie pointed out.

"I don't think so!" Evan scowled, but the remark got another laugh from the other kids.

Will You Be My Valentine?

As Stephanie turned to throw the ball to someone else, she heard Rachel's voice loud and clear.

"I told you that Michelle's party would be a disaster!"

Stephanie froze. Even though her juggling act hadn't been very impressive, Rachel's comment was mean. It wasn't Michelle's fault that Stephanie had run into so many problems or that the class hadn't collected enough money to pay for Marvelous Manfred.

But somehow Stephanie had to turn the floundering party into the smashing success she had promised Michelle. There was only one way to do that.

It was time for the grand finale.

MICHELLE

Chapter
13

Michelle fumed as Stephanie fled the room. Rachel had no right to insult Stephanie's party! When Mrs. Yoshida stepped out to dump the trash, Michelle lashed back in her sister's defense. "The party's not a disaster, Rachel! Everybody's having a great time."

"Oh, really?" Rachel looked around. "Is anyone here having fun?"

Mandy raised her hand. "I am!"

Cassie turned around. Blotches of yellow, blue, and green paint dotted her cheeks and chin. "Me, too!"

Michelle mouthed a thank-you to the two girls.

"You two don't count!" Rachel huffed. "You're Michelle's best friends."

"I thought Stephanie's juggling act was funny," Erin said. "In a weird kind of way."

"Yeah!" Michelle glared at Rachel. "It was *supposed* to be a comedy act!"

Rachel sneered. "But Stephanie *said* she was going to get Marvelous Manfred."

Michelle didn't know why Stephanie hadn't been able to get the famous juggler for the party, but she knew there had to be a good reason. The important thing was that Stephanie had tried really hard to do everything she had promised.

"Can *you* juggle two tennis balls, Rachel?" Michelle asked.

"No, but that's not the point. If you had a mom—"

"Tra-laaa!" Rachel was cut off as Stephanie leaped back into the room with her arms out like a ballerina.

Everyone gawked.

"I am Cupid," Stephanie said. "I am here to make your Valentine's Day complete!"

Michelle blinked in disbelief. Stephanie looked like a ballerina—a really *fat* ballerina—in a padded leotard. A huge fake safety pin was attached to the front of the large diaper Stephanie wore around her bottom. A case full of arrows was strapped to Stephanie's back, and she carried a bow and a grocery bag! The little wings attached to the back of the leotard flopped. She wore a leafy green wreath over her blond hair and her regular hightops on her feet.

All the kids burst into howls of laughter.

Michelle kept staring as Stephanie twirled. What happened to the boy Stephanie had hired to play Cupid? He must have backed out at the last minute, Michelle thought, and Stephanie had taken his place. Just so the class wouldn't be disappointed!

The leafy wreath almost fell off when Stephanie bowed. She pushed it back onto her head and stood up again to face her laughing fourth-grade audience. Her little wings flapped every time she moved.

Michelle glanced around the room. Rachel was the only person who wasn't totally enjoying Stephanie's Cupid routine. Lucas and Ronald were doubled over with laughter. Lee was laughing so hard, he had to take off his glasses to wipe his eyes. Erin got the hiccups.

"What? Haven't you ever seen a teenage girl make a total fool of herself before?" Stephanie teased. She struggled to keep a straight face.

"Not like this!" Anna had almost stopped laughing, then broke into hilarious giggling again.

"My sister wouldn't be caught dead in that outfit!" Karlee yelled from the back of the room.

"Well, neither would I!" Stephanie twirled with her chin up, her arms out, and one of her legs bent back at the knee. She suddenly froze in the comical position and grinned. "But then—I'm not dead! Tra-laaaaa!"

Everyone laughed harder. Even Mrs. Yoshida laughed aloud when she came back in and saw Stephanie's costume.

Michelle grinned at Rachel. "Do you know any *moms* who'd do *that*?"

For a change, Rachel didn't have a cutting

comeback. She sat down, folded her arms, and pouted.

"What does this Cupid guy do anyway?" José asked.

"Do?" Stephanie blinked but she kept her pose.

Michelle scanned the room as the laughter died away. Everyone seemed eager to hear what Stephanie said next.

"I mean, you've got a bow and arrow, but you don't exactly look dangerous." José shrugged.

Hardly! Michelle agreed. She giggled as Stephanie relaxed her pose and made a show of adjusting her diaper.

"Oh, but Cupid is *very* dangerous!" Stephanie's eyes gleamed with delight as she took a fake heart-tipped arrow out of the case. She put the arrow in the bow with a dramatic flourish, then crept toward José.

A tense hush fell over the room.

"Better beware, José! Cupid can make you fall in love!" Stephanie looked around, then pointed. "With Rachel!"

"Oh, give me a break!" Rachel snapped.

José gasped. "But I like Erin!"

The whole class started laughing again.

Erin blushed. "Oh, my!"

José buried his face in his hands.

Stephanie stopped and frowned at the class. "Love is *not* funny. It's the most wonderful feeling in the world!" With that, she did a bunch of funny twirls and turns, then stopped in another silly position.

She held out the bow and arrow and panned the room like she was looking for someone to zing.

Michelle realized Stephanie was trying to distract the class from José and Erin's embarrassment. Her sister was just *too* cool.

The boys threw up their hands in mock protest or ducked under their desks. The girls waved Stephanie away.

"Doesn't *anyone* want to fall in love?" Stephanie asked.

"No!" the class shouted in unison.

"Okay." Stephanie straightened up and put the arrow back in the case.

All the kids heaved a sigh of relief. Stephanie started to put the bow on the floor, then glanced around the class again.

"You're *sure* you don't want to fall in love?"

"Yes!" everyone yelled.

"But it's Valentine's Day!" Stephanie hung her head and faked a pout. "What's a cupid supposed to do if nobody wants to fall in love?"

"Shoot a target?" Jeff suggested.

"Dance some more!" Anna stood up and twirled.

"I know!" Stephanie widened her eyes and held up her finger. "I can pass out some really nifty valentines! Tra-laaaaaa!"

"Tra-laaaaaa!" Half the class echoed the singsong phrase.

Michelle was thrilled. Stephanie's comical Cupid act was a huge hit! Michelle had known Stephanie would do everything she could to throw a dynamite class party, but this was turning out better than she had dared to imagine!

She was so glad, she couldn't wait to repay Stephanie—as soon as Kevin showed up to be her perfect valentine!

Uh-oh. *Kevin!*

Michelle looked at the clock and inhaled.

Will You Be My Valentine?

Ten minutes to four! Kevin would be here any minute! She had to tell Stephanie to get out of that ridiculous costume . . . and quick! She glanced around the room—and gasped.

Michelle withered in her chair when she saw Kevin standing in the doorway.

He was staring at Stephanie.

Who was frolicking around the classroom dressed as Cupid! Dressed as a fat baby in a diaper!

Michelle squirmed. This was definitely not the way to meet your perfect valentine date.

Chapter
14

Stephanie was amazed, and not just because Michelle's classmates loved her Cupid antics. Now that she had gotten over her initial embarrassment, she was having fun! It was impossible *not* to be a clown while wearing a huge padded leotard with a diaper attached.

Even if she hadn't been enjoying herself, Michelle's overjoyed smile made all her efforts worthwhile. In spite of all the problems she had run into, she had given the class a terrific and unforgettable Valentine's Day party.

"Tra-laaaaaa!" the kids sang back.

Will You Be My Valentine?

It took every ounce of Stephanie's self-control not to burst out laughing when the class mimicked her. They were having fun!

Feeling great, Stephanie skipped over to the grocery bag filled with the homemade valentines. She froze as she leaned over to pick it up. This time she didn't strike a comical pose on purpose. She was frozen in shock.

A totally cute boy with light brown hair was staring at her from the doorway!

And I'm wearing a chubby cherub costume and acting like a complete idiot!

When the boy caught her eye, he smiled and waved.

Mortified, Stephanie whirled to face the class. The boy looked vaguely familiar, but she couldn't place him. Did he go to her school? If he did, her life was over! There was no way *anyone* could keep quiet about seeing an eighth-grade girl playing Cupid. Once Judy Morton found out about it, everyone would know!

Oh, no! Stephanie thought. *This is not happening!*

Stephanie stared at the eager fourth-grade

faces—all the kids were waiting for her to continue.

She wanted to run back to the rest room and hide, but she couldn't disappoint the kids.

Or Michelle.

Not even if the gorgeous guy in the doorway thought she was a complete freak.

So maybe she'd be ridiculed forever, Stephanie thought. She was Cupid, and she had a job to do.

Stephanie pulled a valentine out of her bag. "Oh! This one is for Ronald! Where's Ronald?"

The boy sitting behind Michelle raised his hand.

"Just a minute, Ronald. I have a thought." Stephanie struck a thoughtful pose and held it.

"Come on, Stephanie!" Mandy yelled. "Do something!"

Erin raised her hand. "I want to see you juggle again!"

"You mean *try* to juggle," Rachel snapped. No one paid any attention to her.

"I liked the tra-la's." Denise spread her arms and sang out, "Tra-laaaaa!"

Stephanie rocked back and forth with exaggerated excitement. "No, I'm tired of singing. I've got a better idea!" It was harder to look happy, act absurdly, and stay focused now that she knew that boy was watching. "Let's play Cupid Says!"

"Is that like Simon Says?" Evan asked.

"Exactly! Except it's Cupid—not Simon." Stephanie paused to make sure she had everyone's attention. "Cupid says, everybody clap!"

While the kids clapped their hands in time with each other, Stephanie shuffled over to Ronald and handed him his valentine. The kids kept clapping while she reached into the bag for another valentine. She looked up as though she was surprised that they were still smacking their hands together. "Oh! Are you waiting for me?"

Several heads nodded.

"Cupid says, stop clapping!" Stephanie grinned as half the kids flopped over on their desks, pretending to be exhausted. Others shook their tired hands.

Although she didn't look at him, Stephanie

was aware of the cute boy's stare. He hadn't taken his eyes off her!

Not that I blame him! Stephanie shuddered. She wouldn't be able to drag her gaze away from a nerd in a Cupid suit, either!

Michelle was staring at her, too—with that sheepish grin she got whenever she was guilty of something.

Stephanie frowned. *Have I missed something?* She looked down to make sure the diaper wasn't falling off the leotard.

"Pssst! Stephanie!" Mrs. Yoshida pointed to the clock. It was almost four.

Thank goodness! Stephanie nodded at the teacher to indicate she understood it was time to wrap up. In a few minutes the party would be over. Then she could go home and lock herself in her room for the rest of the school year.

Or the rest of my life! she thought.

Stephanie picked up the pace and played a faster version of the Cupid Says game while she handed out the remaining valentines. She didn't look at the boy in the doorway again. His gaze was totally unsettling. She was sure he'd eventually get around to making some sort of comment about her.

When Stephanie finished handing out the valentines, Mrs. Yoshida called the class to order. "I think we all owe Michelle's sister a very big thank-you for a wonderful party!"

"Right on, Stephanie!" Michelle raised two victorious fists in the air. Stephanie smiled as everyone gave her a big round of applause.

Rachel slouched in her chair, Stephanie noticed, scowling.

All right! Mission accomplished!

Mrs. Yoshida grinned at Stephanie as the class whistled and cheered. "I don't think I've ever had this much fun at a class party, Stephanie!" the teacher said.

"Me, either, Mrs. Yoshida." Stephanie treated her enthusiastic audience to another twirl and funny pose. Then, following a final "tra-laaa," she left the room.

Let me out of here! Stephanie thought. She couldn't stand being in this ridiculous costume another minute!

But as she turned to bolt for the door, she was surrounded with kids.

"Can I have your autograph?" Erin held out a pencil and a torn piece of notebook paper. "You are *so* funny, I just know you'll be famous someday."

Stephanie signed the paper. "Thanks, Erin, but comedy isn't what I was thinking of for a career."

Lee tugged on her arrow case. "If you host the Thanksgiving party next year, will you dress up like a turkey?"

"Only if you promise not to roast me." Stephanie grinned.

"Do you have any punch left?" Jamar asked. "That's the best punch I ever had."

"Sorry, Jamar. It's all gone." Stephanie noticed Michelle in back of the crowd. She was jumping up and down, trying to get her attention.

"I have to talk to you!" Michelle looked frantic.

"Later!" Stephanie said.

Mrs. Yoshida came to her rescue. "Come on, everyone. Let's get the room picked up and everything put away."

Stephanie made a beeline for the door as

her fans returned to their desks. The boy was still standing there, grinning! And he didn't step aside even though Stephanie obviously wanted to leave!

"Hi, Stephanie! I'm Kevin Logan and—"

"Excuse me, please," Stephanie mumbled.

"Oh, sure." Nodding, Kevin stepped back. "I love your outfit," he added.

That does it! Stephanie didn't care if it was rude. Cheeks flaming with embarrassment, she barged past the boy and ran down the hall toward the rest room.

"Stephanie, wait!" Michelle called behind her.

But Stephanie just ran faster. This was the most embarrassed she'd been in her entire life!

MICHELLE

Chapter
15

Michelle's heart sank as she watched Stephanie run down the hall. Her sister was holding the wreath on her head to keep it from falling off. The case of arrows and the little wings flapped against her back. The padded diaper jounced up and down. If things weren't such an awful mess, Michelle would have laughed.

She slumped with a dismal sigh instead.

Everything had been going so great! The party was a huge success—and she had found Stephanie a wonderful date for the Valentine's Day party.

Will You Be My Valentine?

Then, wham!

Everything had gone *totally* wrong!

Michelle wouldn't have told Kevin to come to the classroom if she had known *Stephanie* was going to be Cupid!

But she hadn't known because Stephanie hadn't told her.

Still, Michelle felt like a complete jerk. Stephanie was embarrassed that a cute boy had seen her making a fool of herself. And Kevin probably thought Stephanie was some kind of weirdo.

"I don't think Stephanie likes me," Kevin said.

Startled, Michelle looked back. She had forgotten Kevin was still standing there. He looked super in jeans and a casual sweater over a button-down shirt. There was something else different about the way he looked, too, but she didn't know what.

"Why would you think that Stephanie doesn't like you?" Michelle asked.

"Because when I tried to introduce myself, she ran away." Kevin shrugged. "Maybe I shouldn't have mentioned the outfit."

"You didn't!" Michelle sagged. "That was the worst thing you could have said."

"I didn't mean anything bad by it." Kevin stared down the empty hall. "Guess I blew it, huh?"

Michelle blinked. "You mean you still want to go to the skating party with Stephanie?"

"Sure." Kevin frowned, bewildered. "Why wouldn't I?"

"No reason," Michelle said. Kevin was a better choice than she had thought. A lot of boys wouldn't want to go out with a girl who clowned around in a Cupid costume.

"How I feel isn't the problem, though," Kevin said. "It all depends on whether Stephanie wants to go with me."

"Uh—" Michelle hesitated. "Stephanie doesn't *know* you're her date, Kevin. She doesn't even know I *found* her a date!"

"She doesn't?" Kevin said, startled.

Michelle shook her head. "I wanted it to be a surprise."

And, boy, did that backfire!

But it wasn't too late to fix things. She just had to explain everything to Stephanie.

"Just stay here, Kevin, okay?" Michelle backed a few steps down the hall. "Don't go away."

"I'll be right here." Kevin leaned against the wall to wait.

"Great!" Michelle turned and raced to the rest room.

Stephanie was sitting on the sink counter, staring at the floor. She was still wearing the Cupid costume and looked totally depressed.

"How come you're not getting changed?" Michelle asked.

Stephanie shrugged. "I just needed a few minutes to unwind. Besides, it's not like I have anywhere to go."

"Yes, you do!" Michelle exclaimed. "It's after four, and the skating party has already started!"

"I'm not going to the skating party, Michelle!" Stephanie's eyes flashed. "And even if I *had* been thinking about going alone, I couldn't possibly go now. The humiliation would be *too* much."

"Huh?" Michelle paused, confused. Sometimes Stephanie was *impossible* to figure out.

"I just can't face being laughed off the rink." Stephanie's shoulders drooped. "I'm already dreading school on Monday."

"I'm lost." Michelle eased back as Stephanie slipped off the counter and began putting her party supplies back into grocery bags. "What are you worried about?"

"That *boy* out there!" Stephanie rolled her eyes and pointed at the door. "After he tells one of his friends at school that I was playing Cupid for your class, everyone will think I'm a total loser! Judy Morton will make sure of it."

"Is that all?" Michelle grinned.

"All?" Stephanie took a deep breath and softened her tone. "Don't get me wrong, Michelle. I had a great time entertaining your class. Especially since Rachel can't tease you about the party, because everyone else loved it."

"That's totally true." Michelle nodded.

"But," Stephanie continued, "I'm not going to set myself up to be the target of everyone's jokes if I can avoid it."

"Nobody's going to make fun of you,"

Michelle said. "Trust me. Kevin won't say anything. He doesn't even go to your school."

"Kevin?" Stephanie dropped Joey's green hat and turned slowly. "Who's Kevin?"

"The boy out there." Michelle thumbed toward the door. "Kevin's your date for the skating party."

"My *what*?" Stephanie's eyes widened.

"Your date!" Michelle grinned. "I found him for you!"

"But I *told* you not to bother." Dazed, Stephanie leaned against the counter.

"I know, but I just *couldn't* stop looking, Stephanie. You were working so hard on my party, and I wanted to do something special for you." Michelle couldn't tell if Stephanie was mad or not.

"You found me a date." Stephanie shook her head as though she didn't quite believe it. "And he's gorgeous."

She isn't mad! Michelle realized. That made her relax a bit. "Kevin just jumped at the chance to go out with you!" she reported.

"I bet." Stephanie turned and stared into the mirror. She took the wreath off and shook out her hair. "But that was *before* he saw me in this stupid costume!"

Michelle had to admit that Stephanie looked pretty weird in the Cupid suit, but she suspected Kevin would like Stephanie no matter what she wore. "I don't think Kevin cares."

"Get real, Michelle." Stephanie put Joey's hat in the grocery bag and set both bags aside. She hesitated, then smiled. "I really appreciate what you tried to do for me, Michelle, but this may not work out the way you hoped. I just don't want you to be disappointed, okay?"

"What does that mean?" Michelle asked, puzzled.

"I'm sure Kevin is a terrific guy, but he didn't bargain for a girl who wears a padded diaper." Stephanie looked away. "So I'm not going to hold him to his promise. It wouldn't be fair."

Michelle was stunned! After all she had done to find Stephanie the perfect date, she was going to turn him down?

"You can't do that, Stephanie!"

"Watch me." Stephanie reached over her shoulder to unzip the Cupid suit.

"But Kevin really, really wants to go to the skating party with you," Michelle protested.

"Right. Gorgeous guys with wonderful personalities and charming smiles do not date girls who sing tra-la and prance around in chubby cherub clothes." Stephanie grimaced as she tugged on the costume zipper. "Help me with this, will you?"

"Sure." Michelle climbed onto the counter so she could reach. "But Kevin's not like other guys."

"Forget Kevin, Michelle," Stephanie said. "Now that he knows what a loser I am, he probably left anyway."

"No, he didn't." Michelle grabbed the zipper tab and pulled. It didn't budge.

"Just hurry up so I can get out of this leotard." Stephanie scratched under her arm. "It itches like crazy."

Michelle yanked the tab harder. The zipper still wouldn't budge.

"Come on, Michelle. Stop fooling around. I've got to get dressed so I can go let Kevin off the hook." Stephanie jiggled. "I certainly don't want him to see me in this thing again!"

"Well, that might be a problem," Michelle said.

"Why?" Stephanie asked.

Michelle winced. "Because the zipper's stuck."

STEPHANIE

Chapter
16

Stuck! Stephanie gasped and glanced over her shoulder. "What did you say?"

Michelle sighed. "The zipper's stuck."

"Please, *please* tell me you're joking, Michelle." Stephanie begged. She lifted a hopeful eyebrow.

"No joke, Stephanie." Michelle grunted as she pulled on the zipper tab again. "It's stuck."

"No! It can't be!" Stephanie groaned. "Now what am I going to do?"

"There's only one thing I can think of." Michelle jumped off the counter. "We'll just have to go back to my class so Mrs. Yoshida can help."

Stephanie loathed the thought of facing Kevin again wearing the Cupid outfit, but she didn't have any choice.

The only alternative is to wear the hideous costume home! Stephanie thought. *And that has zero chance of happening.*

"Okay." Stephanie sighed in surrender. "Let's go ask Mrs. Yoshida for help."

Holding her chin up, Stephanie followed Michelle out the door and back up the hall. Kids and parents were filing out of the classroom.

Whoa. Stephanie thought. Kevin *was* still waiting by the door!

When Michelle waved, he walked toward them.

"Hi, Kevin!" Michelle greeted the boy with a smile. "This is my sister, Stephanie."

Kevin smiled and started to say something.

Stephanie felt so self-conscious in the Cupid costume, she didn't give him a chance to talk. "Look, Kevin, I know why Michelle asked you to come here, but I'm not going to the skating party with you."

"But why—" Kevin's smile faded.

"I don't know *how* she talked you into being my date"—Stephanie cast a sidelong glance at Michelle—"but you don't have to go through with it."

"But I—" Kevin began.

Stephanie continued without pause. "I know I look totally ridiculous in this stupid costume, which I wouldn't be wearing except for Michelle's party, but—"

"I know, Steph—"

"First impressions *are* the most important." Stephanie knew she was babbling, but she couldn't stop. It was her only defense against the painful truth. If she stopped talking, she was sure Kevin would agree with her and leave.

He was so cute that she really didn't want him to leave. "And I haven't exactly made a great first impression, have I?"

"Yes, you—"

"Memorable, maybe," Stephanie said. "But not—"

Kevin glanced at Michelle.

"Stephanie!" Michelle said. "Would you *please* stop interrupting and let Kevin talk? At least for a few seconds!"

"Sure." Feeling even more self-conscious, Stephanie folded her arms. *Here it comes.*

"Stephanie, I think you're terrific," Kevin said.

Stephanie almost fell over. That was *not* what she expected to hear! "What?"

"Really!" Kevin grinned. "You cared enough about Michelle to host her party when no one else could do it."

"Not to mention dressing up as Cupid," Michelle added. She winced. "Sorry."

"No, don't be sorry! You're absolutely right, Michelle. I think it's great that Stephanie did all this just for you." Kevin looked Stephanie straight in the eye.

Stephanie stared back into Kevin's brown eyes. Michelle was right. He wasn't just incredibly cute, he was nice, too. She didn't have a clue where Michelle had found him, but he was *exactly* the kind of boy she wanted to hang out with.

"You know, Stephanie," Kevin went on, "there aren't many girls who have the self-confidence to wear a silly costume just to make a bunch of kids laugh."

Stephanie blushed, too flustered to speak.

"There aren't many girls who would look as cute as you do in a Cupid costume, either," Kevin added with a shy smile.

"I'm glad you think that," Michelle said. "Because Stephanie can't get out of it."

"What?" Kevin asked.

"The, uh—zipper's stuck." Stephanie pointed over her shoulder.

"Maybe I can help." Kevin stepped behind Stephanie and wiggled the tab.

"I hope so," Stephanie said, "because you don't really want to go roller-skating with Cupid, do you?"

"Honestly? No. I'd rather not." Kevin laughed. "So does that mean we still have a date?"

"Well, maybe," Stephanie said. "There's something I want to know first." She looked at her sister. "Michelle, how did you find this wonderful guy?"

"It wasn't easy!" Michelle exhaled. "I almost *didn't* find anyone. The boys that answered my personal ad were all wrong—"

"Your ad?" Stephanie blinked.

"Yeah! In your school newspaper!" Michelle exclaimed. "I got about a hundred e-mail replies! It took me forever to read them all."

Stephanie's head swam. She couldn't believe how determined Michelle was to find her a date. And she had apparently gone to a lot of trouble.

"So where *did* you find Kevin?" she asked. "The mall? Mail-order catalogue? Or did he put an ad in the school newspaper, too?"

"That's not really my style," Kevin said. He wiggled the zipper tab, then gently tugged it.

"Actually, I found him on the front porch." Michelle giggled. "He's our paperboy."

"No way!" Stephanie exclaimed. How could she have seen Kevin almost every day and not realized he was gorgeous?

"Honest," Michelle said. "It's really weird, but I didn't notice how cute and nice Kevin was until yesterday."

"There! Got it!" Kevin patted Stephanie's

shoulder. "The zipper should work okay now."

"Thanks, Kevin." Stephanie turned. "But now I really am embarrassed. I can't believe I didn't recognize you! You've been delivering our newspaper for months."

"It's the baseball cap." Kevin glanced upward. "That I'm *not* wearing today."

"I knew there was something different!" Michelle squinted at Kevin. Then her eyes widened. She pointed at a clock on the wall. "You guys better get moving, or the skating party will be over before you get there!"

"I'd really love to take you, Stephanie," Kevin said.

"Great!" Stephanie grinned. "Because I really want to go with you, Kevin."

"Well, I'm sure glad *that's* settled." Michelle pulled on Stephanie's diaper. "Come on. You have to get changed."

"Be right back." Stephanie smiled at Kevin as Michelle dragged her toward the rest room.

As soon as they were inside, Stephanie threw her arms around Michelle and gave her a huge hug. "Thank you, Michelle. For the best valentine a sister ever had."

"And thank you for the best class Valentine's Day party a sister ever had." Michelle hesitated, then asked, "So you really do like Kevin?"

"He's great!"

Stephanie laughed. Judy Morton would die of envy when she walked into the roller rink on Kevin's arm. "I am so impressed. You actually found the perfect date for me, Michelle!"

"I did, didn't I?" Michelle grinned. "Maybe *I'm* the one who should be wearing the Cupid costume!"

"Well—" Stephanie's eyes twinkled. "As soon as I get out of it, *you* can have it, sister!"

WIN LOADS OF
COOL PRIZES FOR
YOU AND A FRIEND!

1 Grand Prize: Two backpacks full of identical arts and crafts items (see rules for details) and one copy each of "Passport to Paris" (for winner and a friend).

25 First Prizes: A copy of Mary-Kate and Ashley Olsen's newest home video, "Passport to Paris."

Complete entry form and send to:
Pocket Books/"Full House Sisters Sweepstakes"
1230 Avenue of the Americas, 13th Floor, NY, NY 10020

NAME _____ BIRTHDATE ____ / ____ / ____

ADDRESS _____

CITY _____ STATE _____ ZIP _____

PHONE _____

See back for official rules

Minstrel ® Books   PARACHUTE

Full House™

Sisters

Sweepstakes

Sponsors Official Rules:

No Purchase Necessary.

Enter by mailing this completed Official Entry Form (no copies allowed) or by mailing a 3" x 5" card with your name and address, daytime telephone number and birthdate to the Pocket Books/ "Full House Sisters Sweepstakes", 1230 Avenue of the Americas, 13th Floor, NY, NY 10020. Entry forms are available in the back of Full House Sisters #6: Will You Be My Valentine? (2/00), #7: Let's Put On a Show (3/00) and #8: Baby-sitters, Incorporated (4/00), on in-store book displays and on the web site SimonSays.com. Sweepstakes begins 2/1/00. Entries must be postmarked by 4/30/00 and received by 5/15/00. Not responsible for lost, late, damaged, postage-due, stolen, illegible, mutilated, incomplete, or misdirected or not delivered entries or mail or for typographical errors in the entry form or rules or for telecommunications system or computer software or hardware errors or data loss. Entries are void if they are in whole or in part illegible, incomplete or damaged. Enter as often as you wish, but each entry must be mailed separately. Winners will be selected at random from all eligible entries received in a drawing to be held on or about 5/25/00. Winners will be notified by mail. The grand prize winner will be notified by phone as well. Odds of winning depend on number of eligible entries received.

Prizes: One Grand Prize: Two backpacks full of identical arts and crafts items (for winner and a friend). Items include: 2 backpacks, 2 "Passport to Paris" videos from Warner Home Video, 2 Girl's Best Friend Club (secret message recorders), 2 Body Art Activity Cases, 2 Friendship Fun packs, 2 Mini-stamper Sets, 2 Fun Pencil Bags, 2 Sketchbooks, 2 buckets of sidewalk chalk, 2 Scenstationary packs, 2 True Girlz accessory packs, 2 True Girlz silver jewelry, 2 25-game travel packs. (Total approx. retail value: $216.00). 25 First Prizes: One copy of Mary-Kate and Ashley Olsen's newest home video, "Passport to Paris" from Warner Home Videos (approx. retail value: $20.00 each).

The sweepstakes is open to legal residents of the U.S. (excluding Puerto Rico) and Canada (excluding Quebec) ages 6-10 as of 4/30/00. Proof of age is required to claim prize. Prizes will be awarded to the winner's parent or legal guardian. Void wherever prohibited or restricted by law. All federal, state and local laws apply. Simon & Schuster, Inc., Parachute Publishing, Warner Bros. and their respective officers, directors, shareholders, employees, suppliers, parent companies, subsidiaries, affiliates, agencies, sponsors, participating retailers, and persons connected with the use, marketing or conduct of this sweepstakes are not eligible. Family members living in the same household as any of the individuals referred to in the preceding sentence are not eligible.

One prize per person or household. Prizes are not transferable and may not be substituted except by sponsors, in the event of prize unavailability, in which case a prize of equal or greater value will be awarded. All prizes will be awarded. The odds of winning a prize depend upon the number of eligible entries received.

FULL HOUSE™
Sisters

If a winner is a Canadian resident, then he/she must correctly answer a skill-based question administered by mail.

All expenses on receipt and use of prize including federal, state and local taxes are the sole responsibility of the winners. Winners' parents or legal guardians may be required to execute and return an Affidavit of Eligibility and Publicity Release and all other legal documents which the sweepstakes sponsors may require (including a W-9 tax form) within 15 days of attempted notification or an alternate winner will be selected.

Winners or winners' parents or legal guardians on winners' behalf agree to allow use of winners' names, photographs, likenesses, and entries for any advertising, promotion and publicity purposes without further compensation to or permission from the entrants, except where prohibited by law.

Winners and winners' parents or legal guardians agree that Simon & Schuster, Inc., Parachute Publishing and Warner Bros. and their respective officers, directors, shareholders, employees, suppliers, parent companies, subsidiaries, affiliates, agencies, sponsors, participating retailers, and persons connected with the use, marketing or conduct of this sweepstakes, shall have no responsibility or liability for injuries, losses or damages of any kind in connection with the collection, acceptance or use of the prizes awarded herein, or from participation in this promotion.

By participating in this sweepstakes, entrants agree to be bound by these rules and the decisions of the judges and sweepstakes sponsors, which are final in all matters relating to the sweepstakes. Failure to comply with the Official Rules may result in a disqualification of your entry and prohibition of any further participation in this sweepstakes.

The first names the of the winners will be posted at SimonSays.com or the first names of the winners may be obtained by sending a stamped, self-addressed envelope after 5/31/00 to Prize Winners, Pocket Books "Full House Sisters Sweepstakes," 1230 Avenue of the Americas, 13th Floor, NY, NY 10020.

Don't miss out on any of
Stephaine and Michelle's
exciting adventures!

FULL HOUSE™

SISTERS

When sisters get together...
expect the unexpected!

A MINSTREL® BOOK

Published by Pocket Books

2012-03